SYBIL LUDINGTON

REVOLUTIONARY WAR RIDER

SYBIL LUDINGTON

for Bethany

**SQUARE
FISH**

An imprint of Macmillan Publishing Group, LLC
120 Broadway
New York, NY 10271
mackids.com

Square Fish and the Square Fish logo are trademarks of Macmillan and
are used by Feiwel and Friends under license from Macmillan.

Our books may be purchased in bulk for promotional, educational, or
business use. Please contact your local bookseller or the Macmillan
Corporate and Premium Sales Department at (800) 221-7945 ext. 5442
or by e-mail at MacmillanSpecialMarkets@macmillan.com.

Library of Congress Cataloging-in-Publication Data
Names: Abbott, E. F.
Title: Sybil Ludington : Revolutionary War rider / E.F. Abbott.
Description: New York : Feiwel and Friends, 2016. | Series: Based on a true
story | Summary: A fictionalized account of the sixteen-year-old girl, trained to
handle a musket, who rode alone over forty miles in New York to bring out the
militia before the Battle of Ridgefield.
Identifiers: LCCN 2015011778 | ISBN 978-1-250-10412-0 (paperback)
ISBN 978-1-250-08034-9 (ebook)
Subjects: LCSH: Ludington, Sybil, 1761– —Juvenile fiction. | Connecticut—His-
tory—Revolution, 1775–1783—Juvenile fiction. | United States—History—Revolution,
1775–1783—Women—Juvenile fiction. | CYAC: Ludington, Sybil, 1761– —Fiction. |
Connecticut—History—Revolution, 1775–1783—Fiction. | United States—History—
Revolution, 1775–1783—Women—Fiction. | Sex role—Fiction.
Classification: LCC PZ7.1.A16 Sy 2016 | DDC [Fic]—dc23
LC record available at http://lccn.loc.gov/2015011778

Frontispiece: Anthony22 at the English language Wikipedia

Originally published in the United States by Feiwel and Friends
First Square Fish Edition: 2017
Book designed by Anna Booth & April Ward
Square Fish logo designed by Filomena Tuosto

5   7   9   10   8   6   4

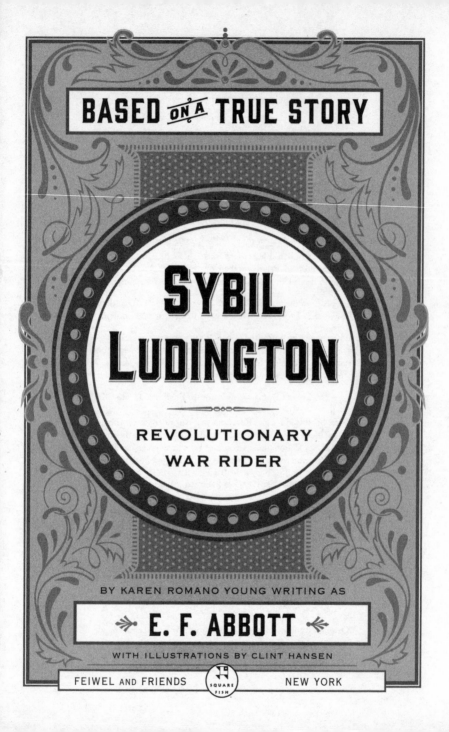

BASED ON A TRUE STORY

SYBIL LUDINGTON

REVOLUTIONARY WAR RIDER

BY KAREN ROMANO YOUNG WRITING AS

E. F. ABBOTT

WITH ILLUSTRATIONS BY CLINT HANSEN

FEIWEL AND FRIENDS   SQUARE FISH   NEW YORK

CHAPTER 1

APRIL 26, 1777

A man rode thundering up the hill on his horse, spattering rain and mud as he galloped directly to the Ludingtons' front door.

In the inner room, lit only by the fire, the family heard him coming out of the dark and moved swiftly to be ready.

Papa stopped rocking the baby. "Take her, please," he said, and passed little Abigail to Mama, her namesake. Mama carried the sleeping baby into the front hall. Papa hovered in the shadows behind Mama. Cradling Abby, she opened the door. "Come in out of the rain, you poor fellow!"

"Message for Colonel Ludington from Colonel Cooke!" the man gasped out.

Papa reached his arm back toward the kitchen. His three daughters hidden there saw his fingers snap, although the sound was covered by his calm, steady voice. "Tell me what you know."

"Danbury is burning, sir! Your regiment is wanted."

As the messenger came in the front, the girls went out the back. Sybil, sixteen, crouched on the porch, unlacing her boots, her dark braid falling over her shoulder. Rebecca, fourteen, held up a pair of boys' breeches. Sybil hopped into them, then pulled her skirt down over the breeches to hide them. Sybil was tall and thin, almost as tall as Mama, with Papa's slate-blue eyes and Mama's high cheekbones. Dressed in those breeches, with her hair bunned up save for one braided ponytail at the neck, she could pass for a boy if she needed to. And she might need to during the long night to come.

Sybil put on a blue woolen militia jacket, turned inside out so only the black lining showed. (There was a johnnycake and a sharp knife already stored in its pockets.) Becky pulled a dark red hood over her sister's hair and knotted its scarf around her throat.

Swift little Molly, eleven, darted across the rain-swept yard to the stable and saddled up Lady Jane as fast as she knew how. She hung a man's tricorn hat across the saddle and draped a shawl over it. The shawl would soon be sopping in this downpour, but it would hide the hat.

On her way back, leading the gray mare, Molly met Papa as he brought the messenger's horse to the stable. "Just water, some oats, and a quick rubdown for this one, my love," said Papa. "The messenger's not staying longer than it takes to eat a bowl of stew."

Papa took Lady Jane's reins. Sybil braced a hand on the horse's shoulder, ready to mount, but Papa held her back. "Did you hear the man?" he asked. "What will be your alarm?"

Sybil straightened, took a breath, then said, "The British are burning Danbury. Muster at Ludington's."

Papa nodded and pulled her close. "Yes! They're coming, and they must be met. We need every single man in the regiment here as fast as he can ride or run."

"You mean as fast as *I* can ride," Sybil said.

The messenger had come out onto the porch and stood, watching. Papa boosted his oldest girl onto the horse's back.

Molly came running back, a strong maple branch in

her hand. She held it up to Sybil. "Don't let anyone near you," she said.

"Don't even get off the horse," said Papa. "Just rap on the doors with the stick."

Sybil tapped her heels against the mare's sides. "Come on, Jane," she said. She left safety behind, with no idea what the night would bring. She went out into lashing wind and cold spring rain, riding among those in this violent corner of New York who might rob her, betray her to enemies, or worse. If she succeeded, her dear papa would be leading his full regiment off to battle come morning. If she failed—what then?

CHAPTER 2

TWO YEARS EARLIER

Colonel Henry Ludington was a traitor, and his wife and children were just as untrustworthy.

That's what the Tories—the people loyal to King George III—around the county said.

"They're right," Papa said. "At least, they've got a right to think so."

Ludington had been on the king's side most of his life, but he had switched sides two years ago when the Revolutionary War began. "It wasn't as sudden on my inside as it looked from the outside," Papa would say, his blue eyes winking—first the left, then the right—at Sybil the way he did when he knew he sounded a little crazy.

Crazy like a fox, thought Sybil, which meant sly and tricky and smart. Crazy the way she wanted to be.

When the first shot of the Revolutionary War was fired on Lexington's town green—"the shot heard 'round the world"—Papa walked away from his Tory friends and didn't turn back.

Sybil was fourteen when that had happened. She was there the day Papa came into the kitchen and stood in the back doorway, leaning heavily against the frame. Mama turned from the fire and met his eyes. "So it's begun," she said.

The minutemen of the Continental Army fire on the British in this depiction of the Battle of Lexington and Concord, 1775. *[LC-DIG-ppmsca-05483]*

Sybil's four little brothers looked up from marching their animals into the wooden Noah's ark and stopped making animal sounds. Sybil and Becky stopped weaving. They let the beaters on their looms fall still and exchanged a meaningful glance.  It took Molly, then nine, to say flatly, "What?"

"The bloodshed," said Papa, too upset to mince words in front of the children.

British soldiers holding Boston—175 miles to the east of the Ludingtons in Dutchess County, New York—had marched on the nearby towns of Lexington and Concord. Two wily leaders of the Patriot rebellion, Samuel Adams and John Hancock, were rumored to be hiding in Lexington. The redcoats, as the British soldiers were called, hoped to get hold of supplies the Patriot militia had stored in Concord—after they'd caught the rebel leaders and strung them up.

"Adams and Hancock knew ahead of time, of course," Papa said.

"How?" That was Molly again, always asking questions.

"General Gage is not as brilliant as he thinks," said Papa gruffly. Gage was the British general in charge of Boston.

"Someone spilled the beans," said Becky. She meant a spy had talked.

"And somebody else picked them up," said Sybil. She meant the message had been passed to the Patriots.

"So they were waiting?" Molly wanted the full story, too impatient to wait for the situation to be drawn out more clearly.

"Two Bostonians were waiting for news of whether the troops were coming by land or sea," said Papa. "One of them—Paul Revere—slipped right under the nose of the big British man-o'-war *Somerset*—that's a ship—and rode all the way to Lexington and on to Concord, to spread the alarm. His friend William Dawes took one leg of the trip, and he took the other."

"How far is that?" asked Sybil.

"At least twenty miles," said Papa. Sybil and Becky raised their eyebrows at each other, impressed.

"Were they in time to call out the militia?" asked Molly.

Papa nodded. He sat down at the table and rubbed his fingers over the wood grain. "But there wasn't much of a militia to drum up," he said. "Old Captain Parker can hardly give the rally cry, he's so weak. He's got eighty-odd farmers for soldiers, so-called minutemen! They haven't got many muskets to speak of. But when somebody fired, they were ready to answer in a minute, all right."

A Patriot defends his home from a British soldier, 1776.
[LC-USZ62-20453]

"How many redcoats?" asked Becky.

"Hundreds, my love," said Papa. "More by the time they got to Concord, but by then, there were more minutemen, too."

"All called out by only two men?" asked Sybil.

"Not exactly. There was a chain of alarm. Some rang bells. People heard and blew horns or conch shells—or lit fires."

This poster encouraged young men to join the troops in the post–Revolutionary War years. [LC-USZ62-51108]

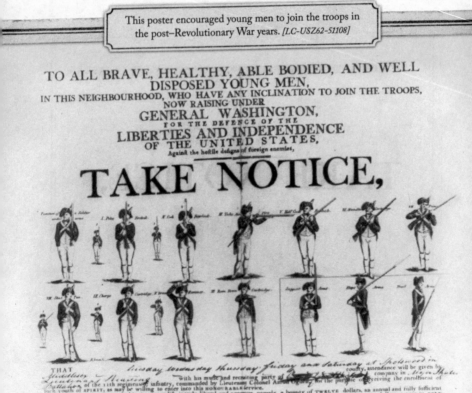

"That worked?" asked Archie. Just seven, he was listening sharp-eared from the floor while his little brothers trotted bears and elephants into the ark.

"It did."

"Then what happened?" Becky chewed a fingernail anxiously.

"Adams and Hancock got away, warned by Revere—who eventually got himself caught." Papa paused, then went on, "The militia marched out to protect their stores, and the redcoats fired on them."

There was a shocked silence.

"How many dead?" asked Sybil.

"More of them than us," said Papa softly.

"'Us,' Henry?" Mama asked.

"Patriots," Papa said firmly. "Colonists. People who came here to have a country of their own."

"We *all* did that," said Becky. "The Loyalists, too. Not just the Patriots."

Mama reached for Becky's hand. "When it comes to guns being fired, you can't be for both sides," she said.

Papa made a little speech then. "I'd rather defend these colonies for ourselves, not for some ruler on a throne thousands of miles away. The so-called Loyalists—the

Tories who call us traitors and rebels—are too scared to oppose him. The British have been getting ready, and now they're gunning us down," said Papa. "It's time for us to get ready, too. *More* ready. Being the readiest—the best prepared—is the only chance the Patriots have got."

"I'm with Papa," said Sybil.

"So am I," said Molly quickly.

"Family business?" asked Papa, placing the palm of his hand on the kitchen table. This signaled that he wanted to keep the matter secret from anyone outside the family. His wife and children circled around him.

"Family business," they answered, and slapped their hands on the tabletop. The decision was made.

CHAPTER 3

"It's time you girls learned to handle a musket," said Papa. His daughters' faces lit up.

In times of peace, any man whose three oldest children were daughters had to turn at least one of them into a son. By the spring of 1776, when war seemed surely to be coming to Dutchess County, it became clear there needed to be *two* people in the family who could manage a musket besides Papa, who might be off doing the work of the war, and Mama, who needed to look after the babies. Two people could take turns on watch, or could defend both the front and back of the house in the event of an attack. Sybil and Rebecca got to be the ones who learned to shoot the best, leaving

Archie to muck out the stalls in the barn and Molly to do most of the milking. But eventually they would learn, too.

Papa took his girls out to the woodland behind the house, a good distance from the road. "Have you decided to let us into your regiment at last?" asked Becky.

Sybil added, "I've heard tell about some girls who dressed as men and went to battle and weren't detected."

"I'd detect you in a minute," said Papa. And he said, as he had said so many times, "No. You won't be soldiers in my regiment, my loves. But you'll be watchmen, in charge of the safety of your mother and sisters and brothers."

He taught them to load, aim, and fire.

They aimed at horse chestnuts set on fence posts and got so they could knock them off the posts at a decent distance. Mama shot, too, brushing up skills

The Brown Bess, a British-made musket used by both sides of the Revolutionary War. [CMH Pub 30-21: American Military History: Volume 1: The United States Army and the Forging of a Nation, 1775–1917]

learned long ago. Molly could fire a musket if it was propped on a fence post (usually by Archie) but you couldn't rely on her to hit a target.

Although Molly wasn't much of a shot, she was good with her hands in other ways. After target practice one night, Molly presented each of her sisters with a small wooden disk on which she had drawn an oak tree—the sign of the Sons of Liberty. But each of their disks  (Molly had made one for herself, too) said DAUGHTER OF LIBERTY. They hung them on black threads around their necks, hidden inside their shifts.

After a month, nobody was a better shot than Sybil; she could even light a campfire with a musket. Soon Sybil and Rebecca had to stop practicing to keep from using up the gunpowder.

"Anyway, girls can't be soldiers." Poor Archie! Never did a boy so want to be a soldier; never was a family so grateful their oldest son was too young to be a drummer boy or even to carry a fife.

Papa said, "George Washington thinks this war will be won with intelligence, not soldiers." It didn't mean being smart, he explained. "The kind of intelligence he needs is secret information."

"The kind you get from spies," added Sybil.

"Can girls be spies?" asked Molly.

"No!" said Archie.

"Why not?" asked Papa. "A spy is like a fox, slipping quickly through the woods, eavesdropping on the mice."

"A gray fox," said Sybil. "Blending in with the branches of the trees." She moved her hands like a fox slipping through the woods.

"Or a red fox," Becky said, shaking back her ginger curls. "Blending in with the fall leaves."

"Mama would make a good spy," said Papa.

Mama rolled her eyes.

"Look at her sweet face. Would you ever doubt a thing she said? Would you ever think she had a trick up her sleeve? But she does. She always has. Remember how she planted a potato on me?"

In the French and Indian War, Papa had served the king of England. He'd fought for the king in 1759 at the Battle of Lake George when he was seventeen, just a year older than Sybil was now.

Papa and his uncles and cousins had traveled from Connecticut to Lake George for the fight. Along the way, they had stopped off in Amenia, New York, to stay with another branch of the family. That was when he first caught a glimpse of Mama, then no bigger than Molly and every bit as smart. Young as she was, Mama hoped Papa wouldn't forget her—and she played a trick on him to make sure he didn't.

Mama had hidden a potato in Papa's knapsack when he went off to fight his battle in Canada back then. It was a potato she and Papa had laughed over in the kitchen at her house. She had stowed it in his knapsack so Papa would find it after he left.

The girls had heard the story before, but Archie didn't recall it, so Papa said, "This potato had a face— two eyes, of course, but also a blobby nose right in between the eyes. Your mama gave it a mouth—"

"—with a row of cloves stuck in—" said Molly.

"—and he carried it all the way to Lake George and back—" said Sybil.

"—singing it sweet love songs," teased Becky.

"That potato kept me company on many a lonely night," said Papa seriously. Then they all laughed, and he laughed, too. "So I took it back to her."

"Wasn't it rotten by then?" asked Archie.

"Well, my love," said Papa, "it had seen better days."

"Don't you want to know what he did to *me* to earn himself that potato?" asked Mama.

"Aw, don't," said Papa. "You were just a little pup. Who could resist?"

"He tied my pigtails to the button on the back of my dress!"

The little boys chuckled.

"That's not all," said Papa, pleased with his younger self.

"No. *Then* he tied my apron to the back of my chair."

The little boys giggled.

"And then, *then*, when they were marching off to war, everyone sniffling and worried—"

"As they should have been," said Papa.

"You know what he did?"

"What?"

Papa couldn't stand it. He took over the story. "There we are, heading off, solemn moment, handkerchiefs waving from the gate, and there's a huge yell—" He squeaked like a stuck pig. "AGH!"

"It was me," said Mama. "And you'd have yelled, too, if suddenly you realized you were tied up to a goat."

"A goat!" the little boys roared.

"He'd tied me to our billy goat by my apron strings, so tight I couldn't turn around to undo them."

Papa was laughing so hard he was crying. "There she is, trying to get away from the goat, and he's trying to butt her, but he's too close to butt her, and the old folks are all sniffling and waving, and she's in a wrestling match with a goat!" Then he pretended to be his young self again, marching off, saluting, before dissolving into laughter again. The children and Mama laughed with him.

They all knew the awful thing that happened next. In the battle, Papa's uncle Amos and his cousin Ezra were killed, dropping wounded as they fought beside him and dying on the battlefield.

That night, alone in his tent, as miserable as he could be, Papa had found the potato, and he knew, if he could just get back to where that girl cousin was, he would be all right.

Papa sobered up telling this part, chucked Mama's cheek, and said, "That potato was like a secret message to me. A person needs to study whatever's in front of him to see what it really is."

"What was the potato *really*, when you studied it?" asked Molly.

"Your mama," said Papa. "With me all the while."

"So are we supposed to study potatoes?" asked Archie.

"No," said Papa. "Spies see through to what the potato stands for. They take second looks at everything."

CHAPTER 4

O nce, long ago, when Sybil was ten, she'd complained about what was for supper. Papa went out in the yard and brought in some bark to set before her. "Papa's just being funny," said Mama. "You don't have to eat bark, children."

"But they could if they had to," said Papa. Then he told the children another one of his war stories.

At twenty, Papa had been given the job of transporting a troop of injured soldiers home from Quebec to Boston. The journey took them all winter. There weren't enough horses. The frozen land of New York and Massachusetts was covered in snow. Anyone who could walk helped the horses haul sleds that carried the ones who couldn't walk. The soldiers dug burrows in the snow to stay warm and ate bark and berries to stay alive.

When she heard that, Sybil ate the bark. "It's delicious!" she told her little sisters and brothers. None of them were sure if sly Sybil really thought the bark was delicious or if she was just trying to prove to Papa that she was tough, too.

Papa took a bite of bark to keep Sybil company. "Mmmm!" he purred, rubbing his stomach. Then he winked at them all with both eyes, first the left, then the right.

When Papa and Mama married and moved to Dutchess County, he left the military. He became a farmer, and for more than a decade, he and Mama worked their land and their livestock and raised a flock of little children.

━━━◦◦◦━━━

But once a soldier, always a soldier, so when Colonel Beverly Robinson asked Papa to be a captain in his regiment, he accepted the post. Colonel Robinson was the master of the farmland that Papa worked. Papa didn't own his land, although he did all the work—229 acres' worth. He had to pay a portion of his income to Robinson. This got on Papa's nerves.

Robinson built Red Mills and made sure his farmers brought their grain there to be milled. He took a portion of the grain as payment. This got under Papa's skin.

Bev. Robinson

Colonel Beverly Robinson was the commander of a Loyalist regiment.
[LC-USZ62-59513]

Robinson's regiment was made up mostly of his tenants. Now Papa was an officer in the regiment, which had been formed to help keep order in the county. And why was order required? Because people didn't like the way Robinson—and all the other British Loyalists—ran things. More and more, Robinson and the Loyalists got up Papa's nose.

Meanwhile, the king of England was also getting on people's nerves and under their skin and up their noses, passing laws asking for more and more money from colonists. Taxes on stamps. Taxes on paper. Taxes on tea. More and more money was demanded from the colonists, and more and more grumbling resulted.

More and more ships full of British soldiers sailed into colonial harbors to "keep the peace." British soldiers in their red coats went marching around the countryside, letting the colonists know who was boss.

Beverly Robinson demanded to know who in his county might be Loyalist and who was—as he put it—a rebel and a traitor. More and more, his soldiers were expected to sniff out whom the king could trust.

Colonel Robinson had hoped Papa would be his strong, tough, right-hand man around the county, making sure that Loyalists were rewarded, so-called Patriots were punished, and fence-sitters were persuaded to choose *his* side of the fence. So Robinson felt extra angry, extra betrayed, and extra spiteful when the war began and Papa wrote a letter to Governor Tryon of the colony of New York, resigning his post.

One day in the autumn of 1775, when Sybil and Becky took the grain to Robinson's mill, they got an earful from several local Loyalists who wanted to make sure Robinson knew where they stood—with the Tories.

"I see who didn't dare show his face around here!"

Private, 1750.   Officer, 1780.   Sergeant, 1807.   Private, 1835.

The evolution of the British infantry uniform from 1750 to 1835.
[Regimental Nicknames and Traditions of the British Army, *Fifth Edition*]

"Good luck to *Captain Ludington*, raising a regiment from these country bumpkins."

"Some people don't know which side their bread is buttered on."

The miller overcharged them, too.

It wasn't that Beverly Robinson was such a popular man. Nobody liked paying his rent. But he represented the well-to-do Loyalists who owned the land and many of the businesses hereabouts. It was what made people fence-sitters, trying to stay on everybody's good side.

Sybil wasn't shy about commenting, "That's ten shillings more than last time."

"And it'll be more yet if I have to hear complaints from you!"

Becky said, "I heard there's a boycott of the shop at Brinckerhoff. Do you know why?"

"Women up there don't want to pay the asking price for tea," said one customer.

"So they're drinking lemonade instead?" asked Becky.

"They ought to be!" said the miller.

"Silly fools. That's good English tea," said another customer. "It's worth any price!"

"*Any* price?" A thin, tall, dark-eyed lady with silver-black hair under her white cap elbowed in: Deborah Carver, the mother of two thin, lanky boys the girls had Sunday school with. She plunked a bag of grain on the miller's counter and chatted, "A hundred women, I heard—wonder if they'll get Abram Brinckerhoff to charge the *legal* price with that many?"

Grumbling rose up, making the Ludington girls glad, but they didn't smile, not until Mistress Carver made one of her typical remarks. "Abram ought to take it or *leaf* it!" She chucked Becky in the side. "Leaves of tea, you see!"

Everybody groaned. Becky giggled. She and Sybil picked up their overpriced flour and slipped off. "Thank you, Mistress Carver!" Sybil said under her breath as they escaped from the mill.

Once they were in the wagon, with Lady Jane's nose pointed toward home, Sybil commented, "That's what Papa means by spy skills. Mistress Carver has them!"

"I like her dumb jokes," said Becky.

"So does everybody," said Sybil. "But think how she took the attention off us—and Papa."

When he heard what had happened at the mill,

Papa frowned, but he smiled about bright Mistress Carver and her tea-leaf joke—and he remembered.

By June 1776, Papa was a colonel himself, with his own regiment in the Continental Army led by General George Washington of Virginia. In July, the Declaration of Independence was written, saying the colonists wanted no more to do with King George III.

Papa announced that the Ludingtons were going to build a mill of their own. "There's no law against it," he said, "and there's plenty of good cause for it." For one thing, it was thirteen miles to Red Mills and back—too far and too unsafe for two girls and a good horse and a cart full of grain. Too bad for Colonel Robinson.

CHAPTER 5

Soon after the Declaration of Independence was delivered to King George, British troops began filling up New York, trying to lay claim to the Hudson River just twenty-five miles west of the Ludington farm.

By August, General George Washington reported to his officers that there were more than thirty thousand British soldiers in New York City.

"How many do we have?" Sybil asked.

"Ten thousand five hundred and fourteen."

It did not escape Sybil's notice that her father—or General Washington, or both—had estimated the British troops, but counted every man of the Continental troops.

"I wish I could join," she said.

"Just you dwell on what you *can* do, my love," Papa said.

Sybil planned to do exactly that.

If the British controlled the Hudson River, they would divide the colonies right through New York, with New England to the northeast and the middle states to the south. If the British tried to come up the river to get the supplies stored along the Hudson,

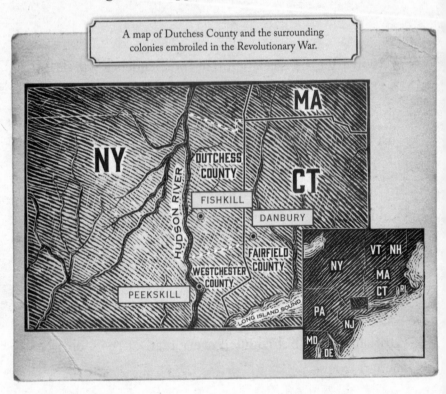

A map of Dutchess County and the surrounding colonies embroiled in the Revolutionary War.

Papa's regiment—and the rest of the Continental Army of New York and Connecticut—were going to have to fight them.

That summer, while the Ludingtons' mill was built, while buckwheat and corn grew tall in the fields, while Lady Jane's foal Poughkeepsie was born and tottered about, secret forces were at work among the people of the county.

Each and every person was deciding where he or she stood—for the king or not.

Regiments formed for both sides, and all of them needed muskets and shot, rifles and bullets, coats and boots, horses and carts, food and drink. Along with the militias of Massachusetts, Connecticut, Pennsylvania, New Jersey, and beyond, Papa and the other colonels swore they'd be ready in a minute, the minute the British showed up.

The disparity in the size of the armies put the Continental Army at a great disadvantage. In August, the British beat Washington badly at Brooklyn, and later in Manhattan. The Ludingtons could feel the redcoats getting ready to march north—and the rest of the county could, too.

Papa was called to a meeting over in Fishkill one

Saturday night with the leaders of other nearby regiments and with General George Washington and a lawyer named John Jay. "General Washington and Mister Jay are scholars," said Papa with awe at Sunday dinner. "They know the histories of secret societies—everyday folk with a talent for learning what's *really* going on, and then passing the word."

John Jay (1745–1829) became the first Chief Justice of the United States. *[LC-DIG-det-4a26384]*

"Do we have *real* spies in our army, Papa?" asked little Hank, who was eight.

"Just real Americans, my love," Papa answered.

The children's imaginations were caught by the idea of spies sneaking around like spiders in their black clothes, leaving coded messages that could be read for dates and times, names and places—which could make the difference between winning and losing the war.

"Spies are watchful," said Tertullus, just four.

"Nobody suspects them," said Derick, who was six.

"They have skills nobody expects them to have," said Archie. He wanted to be like that.

⟞⟞◦◦◦⟝⟝

Sybil had a secret she was sure her family did not know. She loved a man named Enoch Crosby, a big-shouldered, shaggy-haired, gray-eyed, and mysterious man who came and went in disguise or by dark of night, and disappeared again the same way, camouflaged among the trees like a gray fox.

All the Ludingtons loved Enoch. They had loved him years ago when they knew him as a traveling cobbler, someone who made and fixed their shoes. Like other traveling workmen, Enoch camped in the woods between towns and farms. Besides his cobbler's fee, he earned kindness—a bed, a meal—from the families he served.

Like most farm families, the Ludingtons weren't wealthy. Shoes were passed down from one child to the next, from Sybil to Tertullus (Abby wasn't old enough for shoes yet). Enoch always seemed to come along just in time to fix a sole or sew a new upper. If it took him a day or two, so much the better for him; he'd have the benefit of a roof and food for two nights, not just one. As for the Ludingtons, they'd get to hear the tales and troubles he picked up along his cobbler's route.

At some point over the last two years, the stories had stopped being just gossip—how so-and-so and what's-his-name were sparking up a romance. At some point, it started being politics—how Governor Tryon had become General Tryon, hell-bent on dominating New York for the British. At some point, it became crime stories—how the Cow Boys had stolen livestock from a traveler on his way to Poughkeepsie, sold it to the Skinners, who "returned" it to the traveler in exchange for "a reward"—his money!

Enoch brought plenty of those kinds of stories; there were more bandits, gangs, and evildoers than ever before.

Enoch did not know that Sybil would have gotten up and gone with him anywhere, ever since she'd met him when she was thirteen and he was making shoes— but even more since last fall when he'd stopped making shoes *for real* and started making them just *for show.*

On a beautiful afternoon last September, Enoch had appeared at milking time and found Sybil bringing the cows down the meadow. She sent Molly to start the milking and lingered to hear what he was up to. "I'm going to join Swartwout's regiment," he said. "The king's men are getting far too comfortable in New York."

"Is Swartwout going to make them uncomfortable?" Sybil asked.

"That's the idea," Enoch said with a grin.

He stayed that night and sewed the flapping sole of the shoe Archie had handed down to Hank. It would be the last of the Ludington shoes fixed by Enoch. He was gone in the morning.

CHAPTER 6

Four days later, Mama took Sybil for a walk in the pumpkin field. "Papa's gone to Westchester to bring a prisoner to the jail in Fishkill," Mama said.

"Some jail," Sybil snorted. The Patriots had had to turn the Dutch church into a jail.

"It's perfect for this purpose," Mama said. "The prisoner is Enoch."

"*What?* Why? What's he done to get put in jail?"

"Sybil," Mama said. She crossed her arms and looked at her feet, then at Sybil, who was the same height. "There's something Papa and I need you to know about Enoch. Don't fuss! He's in good enough health, but he's in some trouble."

"You're not about to tell me Enoch is some kind of villain. A Cow Boy or something like that. Because I'll never believe it."

"Careful what you say now," said Mama. "Careful who might hear. I tell you this only because I know how much you"—she paused—"*care* about Enoch Crosby."

Sybil crossed her arms, too. "I already know he's joined the army."

Mama said, "He *planned* to join Captain

George Washington (far left) and Harvey Birch (with material draped over both arms) in an illustration from James Fenimore Cooper's novel *The Spy*. The character of Harvey Birch is reportedly based on Enoch Crosby. [LC-USZ62-112531]

Swartwout, but the regiment marched for White Plains before he got there. So he followed their trail to catch up. In the woods, he came upon other campers— a man named Bunker, who was going to join the British army."

Sybil stared. "So this Bunker found out he was a rebel and captured him?"

"No. Enoch let Bunker speak first—you might try that yourself, Sybil. When he realized where Bunker was headed, he pretended *he* was, too."

"So Bunker thought Enoch was a Loyalist?" Sybil gave a nervous laugh.

"They camped together that night. In the morning, they went their separate ways. By then Enoch had learned where the British were mustering and where they planned to go."

Smart, foxy Enoch!

Mama went on, "And he carried the intelligence to Captain Townsend." Townsend was a Patriot who wanted nothing more than to hunt down Loyalists and make them pay—in supplies, in ammunition, in their own lives. He turned things upside down for Enoch. "Townsend asked him to find out more. He said Enoch was of more value as a spy than a soldier."

A spy? Enoch? "Then what?" Sybil's breath was short, though they were walking slowly along the rows of pumpkins.

"Townsend pretended to let him escape. Enoch ran to Bunker, and turned the tables—he gave *Bunker* news about *Townsend*."

Sybil rubbed her forehead. "False news?"

"No, something true. If it was false, they'd see through him too fast."

Sybil groaned. "I don't understand!"

Her mother made her see: Enoch had to pretend to be a British spy sneaking around gathering intelligence about the Patriots. That way the British would trust him, and he'd be able to get intelligence about *them* for the Patriots.

"Well, if he's trusted on both sides, then why is he in jail?"

"To show the British that the Patriots think he's their spy. He has to go to trial first, and be sentenced to jail by the Patriots."

Sybil shook her head.

Mama went on, "He'll be guilty. He'll go to the jail in the church."

Sybil was beginning to understand. "So Papa's

going to guard him in jail and keep the British from coming to rescue him?"

"And what else do you think, my wise girl?"

Sybil stood still for a moment, then answered, "And let him out in secret?"

"Something like that," said Mama.

———◦◦◦◦———

Under the dark of night, while Papa's militiamen kept watch over the Dutch church jail in Fishkill, a lone figure pushed a makeshift bar away from an upper-story window, climbed down the ivy to the ground, and stole away. Three mornings later, Sybil found Enoch asleep in the barn, in the spare stall near the two oxen, Chess and Checkers. He didn't look anything like a fox—more like a bear, with dark thick hair and heavy shoulders. "You know what happened?" he asked without even saying hello.

She nodded.

"You have to act like you know that I've gone over to the enemy side. Another turncoat. Another traitor."

"I know better than that!" said Sybil fiercely.

"My parents don't," he told her.

"They think you're a Loyalist spying on the Patriots?" she whispered, realizing what a dangerous secret
she was being asked to share.

"I'll serve as I'm needed," he said. "Who knows
what kind of messages I'll have to carry? Who
knows what I could find? It could be the difference
between winning and losing the war."

"Great," she said bitterly.

"It *could* be great," Enoch said. "And I know it
means as much to you as it does to me. You'd do

anything, Sybil, wouldn't you, to see this country free? *Our* country free?"

"What good is it, if you have to be some terrible person spying on your own people?"

His gray eyes filled. "I won't be a terrible person as long as you know I'm not," he said. "And I'll be here when I can be. So I want you to do two things for me, Syb. No, three things. First, look for your *own* chance. That'll help you understand why I'm taking this chance for myself to do what I can for the country it's *going* to be when all this is over, however many more years that's going to take.

"Second, the drum your father has on the back porch, lying on its side?" It was an old drum saved from the French and Indian War. "There's going to be plenty of people coming through here. Loyalists carting supplies. Militiamen and strangers. If the coast is clear, stand the drum on its end—straight up—and I'll know it's safe to sleep here."

She pictured Enoch's new life, slipping into the woods, passing messages and telling made-up stories and having people think bad things about him.

"I will stand the drum up," she said. "But what's the third thing?"

He reached for her hand. "Find someone to spark up a match with," he said.

She tore her hand away. "What are you talking about?"

He folded his hands in front of his chin, hiding his mouth. "You can't think of me that way anymore."

"Who says I do?"

"Nobody," he said. "Only consider it a disguise, a mask. A girl like you—tall, lovely—people will wonder if you don't have someone."

That was the thing that made Sybil cry. Since she wouldn't let him see her do that, she rose and strode away from the stable.

CHAPTER 7

On a Sunday morning in December, Becky took a little walk with Eleazar (he went by Leazar) Hazen before Sabbath worship. Sybil stopped Molly from tagging along with them. To get back at Sybil, spiteful Molly told Mistress Hamblin that Sybil was sweet on young Timothy Carver. After that, everybody at the worship meeting looked differently at Sybil.

Both Barnabas and Timothy Carver were tall, bony, pale boys with stringy black hair and pimply skin. Barney and Timmy Carver and Leazar and his brother Moses Hazen were all privates in Papa's regiment. Barney was funny and lively like his mother. But Timmy was lovesick—for Sybil. Along with Leazar, he conspired to sit with the Ludington girls at Sunday worship and hung around Sybil while the congregation socialized before and after the meeting—and any other time he saw her.

Sybil had already been annoyed at being paired with Timmy in people's minds just because he was the only boy taller than she was. Since joining Papa's regiment, he had begun saying politely, "Please call me Timothy." But, as Sybil said, "He's too much a Timmy." This morning, he had sat next to her all through the worship meeting, whispering in her ear and plucking imaginary dust off her sleeve.

"The least you could do is call him what he wants," Becky said. Becky was happy to help Molly tease Sybil, as handsome Leazar Hazen's strong shoulder bumped against hers. Becky hoped nobody noticed when he tugged at one of her red curls then let it bounce back up.

Leazar had been coming to the Ludingtons' Sunday dinner since the summer. Other mothers were always saying things to Mama along the lines of "It won't be long," or "That's a fine match," or "Some fine spark there." It might be easier for Becky and Leazar to be married if Sybil would hurry up and find someone herself.

"What was *Timothy* telling you about, anyway?" Becky asked, jiggling Sybil's elbow.

"He was telling me about duck hunting," said Sybil, and everybody laughed.

Leazar said, "It's quite a fine art, to hear Timmy tell it."

"Timothy," said Becky.

Sybil said, "You have to be very quiet and think like a duck."

They all howled.

Molly said, "If I hadn't told Mistress Hamblin that Sybil was sweet on Timmy, she might have kept on speaking ill of the regiment."

Mama tsked. "Molly, you didn't."

"Oh yes she did," said Sybil. "Right in front of both Timmy and me!"

"What did Mistress Hamblin say about the regiment?" asked Papa.

"Only that the ladies would have something to say about it if too much of the wool they were spinning this winter got dyed blue for militia coats," said Molly.

"What did Timmy—*Timothy*—say?" asked Mama.

"He said they'd fight just as hard with or without coats—and that if they had to fight in homespun, they would blend in with the woodlands better than redcoats!" said Sybil.

"Quite a serious remark," said Mama.

"He's quite a serious Timmy," said Molly, giggling until Papa pulled her ear.

"They'll get you back, these sisters, when it's your turn to spark with a boy," he said.

Molly recoiled. "I'm not interested in *boys*," she said.

Then Papa told them all, "You have to be careful what you say to Loyalists, girls."

Becky huffed. "Mistress Hamblin is nobody to worry about."

"All the more reason to be careful," Mama said sternly. "She tries to *make* herself somebody to worry about."

The four hundred militiamen in Papa's regiment lived spread out over more than a dozen square miles of countryside—and the Carvers were just about at the outer limit. "Getting a message to the Carvers is going to be a problem," said Papa.

Passing messages was a tricky business even close by. You couldn't race around as if there was a fire somewhere; a suspicious Loyalist was bound to stop any known Patriot—or his daughters—who looked as though he or she was spreading an alarm.

After Leazar was gone, Mama sat her three

daughters down. "Tongues are wagging about you and Timmy, Sybil," she said. "How do you feel about that?"

"How *should* I feel?" asked Sybil.

Becky said loyally, "She doesn't care for Timmy the way she"—she stopped herself—"the way he does for her."

Sybil was relieved that nobody mentioned Enoch.

"She'll have to fight Timmy off," said Molly, giggling again.

"Molly," Mama said. "You shouldn't tease her so." She studied Molly, then looked seriously at the others, as if asking herself some question. "Imagine that Sybil really *was* in love with Timmy," she said.

"Mama!"

"Would you tease, Becky? Would you be their messenger, Molly? Would you encourage Timmy, Sybil?"

All the girls' mouths were open.

"What if pretending that way would help Papa call out the regiment?" asked Mama.

"Timmy's not pretending," Becky said.

Sybil was sitting on her hands, anxious and confused—but eager to have a bigger role. Was this the sort of game that Enoch had had in mind when he told her to watch for her chance? "I'd rather be a guard or a militiaman," she said grimly.

By mid-December, it began to be known that the Ludington girls were both courting—slim, dark Sybil with young Timothy Carver (not much to look at, but a reliable lad) and rosy, red-haired Rebecca with Leazar Hazen. They formed a handsome little set at Sunday meeting, sharing Bibles between them.

One Bible was Deborah Carver's (Timmy's mother). The other belonged to Mama.

A closer look at each of them would have revealed small penciled notes in the margins.

Becky and Leazar smiled, whispered plans and compliments, and taught each other a code they could use to send each other notes. In their code, the alphabet was shifted a few letters over. How many letters over was shown in the number of hearts drawn along the edges.

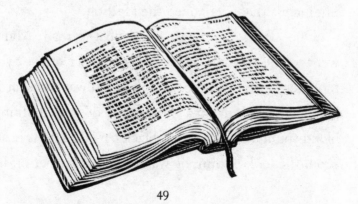

Timmy and Sybil compared lists of numbers and words, pointing out notes in their mothers' Bibles (written at home with the help of their fathers on Saturday night).

$711 = GW$ and $193 = fleet$ were just two examples of what could have been seen there had anyone spied.

By the week before Christmas, Becky and Leazar had perfected a code for notes sent north (the Ludingtons) to south (the Hazens), and Timmy and Sybil had a plan for getting word from east (the Ludingtons) to west (the Carvers).

The Continentals, led by Washington, had been forced out of New York City, across New Jersey, and into Pennsylvania. It seemed likely that the British would storm up the Hudson. Washington sent word to Papa's regiment and some others to come defend the Highlands that overlooked the Hudson.

One afternoon, a cart came up the road. Mama went to the window, baby Abigail in her arms. Sybil took her position in the shadowed hallway, musket in her hand, while Mama opened the door. A hulking, blond young man stood, his black hat still on his head. From the look of him, he was a Quaker farmer on his

This drawing is meant to be a comical depiction of a Quaker meeting, circa 1678–1679. [LC-USZ62-5808]

way back to Quaker Hill, which was along the road that ran east toward Fredericksburg.

"Will you stop in for a warm drink, friend?" asked Mama.

"I thank thee, no, ma'am," said the man. "Mistress Ludington? I am Peaceable Moon."

Sybil smiled and let go of the musket. He wasn't much older than she was, though he was twice her size. The Quakers were known for being neutral and for being—as the man's name said—peaceable.

"I have a note for Miss Rebecca Ludington," he said.

Leazar had dared to send his first love note with news from the south. There were little pictures of Christmas holly and gingerbread men and five hearts in the margin. That meant a five-letter shift, so that code letter *A* stood for *W*, *E* stood for *A*, and so on, as in this key:

a	b	c	d	e	f	g	h	i	j	k	l	m	n	o	p	q	r	s	t	u	v	w	x	y	z
e	f	g	h	i	j	k	l	m	n	o	p	q	r	s	t	u	v	w	x	y	z	a	b	c	d

CODE:

The drawings were a good distraction, but the message was serious—and surprising—and it was good news.

> *Sweet Beck,*
> *aewlmrkxsr xeoiw xvirxsr erh tvmrgixsr mr ria*
> *nivwic.**
> *Your Leazar*

When Papa came home, in time for the New Year, the Ludingtons toasted his regiment—and General Washington and his victories at Trenton and Princeton. "Victory or death!" said Papa, raising his mug of ale.

---

* Washington takes Trenton and Princeton in New Jersey.

CHAPTER 8

Earlier in December, before he led his regiment to the Highlands, Papa had taken Sybil inside and shown her a letter John Jay had written. The letter was to be delivered to Enoch's parents in case Enoch was killed. Papa showed it to Sybil, in case *he*—Papa—died. The letter said that Enoch had really been a Patriot all along. Mister Jay asked Enoch's parents to give their good son a Patriot's burial and to forgive him for the mask he had worn during his life.

For now, Enoch's parents wouldn't let him in their house. How could they forgive what couldn't be explained? Sybil had stood the regiment's drum on the porch before Christmas, in the hope that Enoch would come to the Ludingtons' now that he couldn't go to his own family.

Since Washington's victories in New Jersey, Mama and her girls had wondered whether the British generals would rally and battle back. When they didn't, it seemed that the whole country breathed a sigh of relief—or exhaustion. Once the British retired for the winter, the regiment came home from the Highlands. They were cold, tired, and hungry but unharmed. The roses came back into Mama's and Becky's cheeks—but Sybil felt empty.

A soft snow fell just after the New Year, keeping most travelers at home. Sybil left the drum standing, just in case Enoch was near. One late afternoon just after sunset, there was a knock at the back door, and Enoch poked his shaggy dark head through.

Although he nodded and smiled at Sybil, he sat down at the table near Papa on the other side of the room, not near the chair where she sat sewing. He didn't seem to have come to be with her but rather to talk plans and strategy.

"If you were the British, what would you want?" asked Enoch.

Well, the children knew that well enough: everything they made or grew. So did General Washington. "Supplies for soldiers," Molly said like a parrot. Anyone who grew or made anything—which was everyone—had to make twice as much, or give up half what they needed for themselves. What they didn't give got taken. Cow Boys stole horses for the British, Skinners stole them back for whichever side bid more, and the Committee of Safety—Papa's men—had their hands full keeping them all in check.

"Gunpowder," Sybil said.

"Guns?" asked Archie.

"Cannons," said Derick.

So Hank said, "Cannonballs."

Enoch said, "Molly's right, really. What the British need most is to keep the Continental Army from getting too strong. If we have guns and ammunition, cannons and horses, uniforms and food, tents and hospital supplies, then we'll be a real army."

"That's what the Battle of White Plains was all about," said Rebecca.

Sybil was angry about the response of the soldiers in some of the Westchester regiments.

Papa said she didn't understand what the soldiers

were up against; Sybil thought the regimentals were short on nerve.

Even the little boys knew the stories: ever since the Battle of Long Island last summer, some Continental militiamen had deserted—running home or just running away.

"If they had tails, they would have been tucked between their legs," Sybil said.

"But it was just good sense, really, when you were faced with thousands of British redcoats in their bright uniforms, with their shining new rifles and deadly bayonets," said Papa.

"It's going to be a big job this winter to be ready for the spring," said Mama.

Putting together a real army had become a priority. There wasn't much to work with. Old muskets got pulled out and polished up, but they still weren't reliable. Their musty muzzles weren't trustworthy in the rain, got sticky in the fog, and complained even when it was cloudy out. And rifles weren't much use without bullets. Continental soldiers in New York went so far as to melt down a lead statue of King George: the statue made 42,000 bullets!

"Who wants to hear about General Washington's Christmas?" Enoch asked of the family as they were at

George Washington greeting the Marquis de Lafayette at Valley Forge, Pennsylvania. *[LC-USZ62-53986]*

work in the weaving room and the kitchen. (Nothing but blue wool—on warp, weft, and weave, on the big loom and the small: jackets for the militia.)

Everybody did. "As you know, the British soldiers appreciate Christmas dinner. And this year they were especially festive, having routed Washington and his men into the wilds of Pennsylvania."

The little boys booed and hissed.

"But General Washington decided not to take a holiday. He rowed across the Delaware River from Pennsylvania in little boats and surprised the British over their Christmas pudding!"

"Hurrah!"

It took Molly to ask the impolite question: "Well, are the British stupid, then?"

"No, more's the pity, my love," said Papa. "This war will be won on who knows more, I think."

"You mean who's smarter?" said Archie.

"In a way. But no. I mean secret information."

Archie lit up.

"How do you *get* secret information?" Molly asked.

"Tell them about C.A.I.R., Colonel," Enoch said.

C.A.I.R. stood for four things that a spy was good at.

C was for *collecting*.

"That's what *you* do, Archie, when you pay atten-tion the way you do," said Papa. "Listening at doors. Listening at the mill. Watching the woods."

"You're collecting intelligence," said Enoch. "And that's what's going to win us this war. That and keep-ing what you learn to yourself."

"Somebody learned where the British were having Christmas dinner," Mama said.

"And how many men were on guard," said Papa.

A was for *assimilation*.

"For *what*?" Archie asked.

"Blending in," said Enoch.

"You're great at that," Sybil told Molly. She sat on the rug cross-legged in front of her sister. "Nobody pays much attention to girls of any size, especially little girls, and not much to little boys."

"I'd rather stand out," retorted Molly.

"Not if you're a spy," said Sybil.

Archie said, "What's the *I* for?"

"Interaction," said Mama. "Talking to people and finding out what they know. Becky is brilliant at that."

"What about *R*?" asked Becky.

"Resolve," said Papa.

"What's that?" asked Hank.

"Refusing to quit," said Papa.

"Never backing down," said Enoch. "And being willing to do things you don't want to do, because they might be the difference between life and death. Sybil's got that."

"I only pretend to," said Sybil, thinking of Timmy. Oh, how she wished there were something she could do with all her heart!

Late the next afternoon, when the sun set on the short winter day and the light faded too fast, Enoch asked Sybil to do something new for him. "I have to be invisible," he said. "You need to forget my name and whatever you used to know about me."

"Now *you're* pretending," said Sybil, disgusted. As if she could ever forget Enoch! "You're pretending you don't care what happens to you."

"Courage is mostly just pretending," said Enoch.

They were on the back porch. Sybil patted her

hands on the skin of the tall drum, making it rumble, avoiding Enoch's eyes.

"These things I've agreed to do are going to make me everybody's enemy."

"You'll never be *my* enemy," she said.

"Then I'll ask you this," he said. "Don't believe anything you hear about me."

Sybil made a face.

"And this. If you're ever unsure, and you don't know who to trust, go see Solomon Hopkins."

Solomon Hopkins! The gray-haired man with the leg wound from the last war was an officer in Papa's regiment, but she didn't see why. He seemed useless to Sybil. He was on Papa's list to wake for a muster, but he was not a militiaman. He came to the mill and picked over every little thing as though his life depended on not having one buckwheat lump in his flour, one husk of oat in his meal.

"Should I stand the drum up if it's safe?" she asked.

"It's not going to be safe," he said. "From now on, some militiaman could arrive here any time of night or day. Don't stand it up again."

A lump formed in Sybil's throat. "Will you send messages?"

"Maybe a potato?" he said. He had known her family long enough to hear that old love story.

Against her will, she smiled.

He said, "Syb, I can't send you any messages without endangering you. Know this"—she looked up to see tears glistening in his eyes—"any message I send is to you."

Right after that was when Sybil taught her little brothers to spit on the ground when they heard Enoch's name. "But we're Patriots!" said Molly. "And so's he!"

"We're spies," said Sybil. "We pretend to hate him because we really love him."

CHAPTER 9

It would have been a fine enough winter if it had been possible to forget there was a war coming. The war seemed to rest under the snow along with the weeds, waiting to sprout again and cause trouble in the spring.

Enoch was right; he wouldn't have been safe at the Ludingtons' with so many regimentals about. The regiment was called upon to smooth the frozen ruts of mud in the road so that wagons loaded with supplies wouldn't break their axles. And when they weren't doing that, they filled the parade ground up the hill, marching, drilling, aiming their muskets, and practicing being ready in a minute.

Leazar spent the late winter at the Ludingtons'

house, teaching fife to Jamie Tomkins and Daniel Townsend and helping the drummers—including Charlie Townsend, Daniel's brother—figure out how to play a military beat. And slipping off for walks with Becky.

In the first week of March, just when it looked as if warm weather might finally come back to Dutchess County, Leazar's father, Caleb, took ill. It had started with a cold, and what with drilling out on the parade ground with the regiment, it turned to bronchitis, with coughing so bad that Papa began urging him to stay home. But he didn't until it was too late. He died of pneumonia just when it began to be spring.

"That poor woman" is what Mama said of Mistress Sarah Hazen. Never the strongest person, and with no daughter, Mistress Hazen had the running of their big farm on her plate, and nothing but toil as a pension. If Caleb had died on the battlefield, she could have claimed a military pension—but now she was in trouble.

And so was Becky. She'd had plans with Leazar, the family was sure of it, but if he married, his military pension would go to his wife, not his mother. Leazar and his younger brother, Moses—both privates in the regiment—did not intend to leave their mother alone now that rumblings were coming from New York City.

Mama and her daughters didn't envy Mistress Carver and the other women whose men spent so much time hereabouts. They loved having Papa home, and they were glad for the color and noise of the soldiers, as well as for the protection. Papa was a wanted man—not just a Patriot leader but a traitorous one—and a target for Tory gangs that would have loved to get their hands on him.

———⟩∘∘⟨———

One warm March evening, the Ludington young ones were let loose to play hide-and-seek in the yard. Archie was winning.

There was just enough pink and blue light—pink from the sunset, blue from the coming night—to see the shape of a nine-year-old, messy-looking, mud-covered, redheaded boy. But nobody could find Archie. It was as if he wasn't there.

The little boys were getting impatient waiting for Archie to turn up. They shuffled their feet and banged one another's elbows, hoping to raise some reaction from Molly by getting in a fight. But that, in turn, would wake Mama, who'd gone to bed with the baby, tired and sneezing. And that, in turn, would bring down the wrath of Sybil and Becky, busy cleaning up from supper and doing the other business of the house. So Molly hissed at them, "Stop!"

Papa had gone to meet with John Jay and George Washington and the other colonels to compare information about the advances the British were sure to make the moment spring sprung.

Molly whispered to her brothers, "Spy for Archie's ginger pigtail." But there was no sign of Archie, nothing to spy, nothing to hear, not even a rustle.

Molly yodeled softly, "All-y, all-y in come free!"

Suddenly a shadow grew legs. Archie came tearing across the yard like a maniac. Molly and the little boys raced toward home base, but Archie shot past it and went right around the house. He fell against the front door, thumping on it with the flat of his hand, a weird, muted way to knock.

Sybil stuck her sharp nose out. "Mama's going to—"

"He skipped home base!" Molly tattled.

Archie grabbed Sybil by the arms and shoved her right inside. "Get in," he commanded. "There's men in the woods."

"Who?" asked Derick, just six years old. "Cow Boys?"

Sybil crossed her arms. "Archibald, you shouldn't be scaring the boys."

"I'm not afraid," said Tertullus.

"You're a brave boy, Turtle," said Sybil.

Archie said, "I don't know who it is, but they're after Papa."

"How many?" Sybil had Archie by the shoulders.

"A dozen, at least. They've got rifles and muskets. I could see them. I could hear them, too. They're already on this side of the brook. They're saying something about Papa and how he's got money on his head. Do they mean under his hat?"

"Wake Mama," Sybil told Becky. "Somebody's after the bounty."

"We've got those jackets sewn," said Becky. "I know what to do."

Moments later, Sybil roughly pushed the boys and Molly out the back door. "You've had your drink. Now don't come in until you're called," she announced in her loudest voice, the voice Papa called the shrew voice. "I've got enough to do feeding *all these hungry militiamen* without having to deal with a bunch of babies!"

Archie kicked at the door furiously. "What's she *talking* about?"

"It's just pretend," Molly whispered. "Don't be afraid."

Derick fussed, "I'm not a baby!"

"And *I'm* not afraid," said Turtle again.

"Good," Molly said. "Then you can be It. Stay here and count as high as you can."

Turtle turned his face to the fence post and covered his eyes. He was still peeking.

"Cheater," Derick couldn't help saying.

"One," said Turtle. "Two."

Archie and Molly continued to play, but they really watched the woods and the house. Sybil was placing lighted candles in the back windows.

"Eight. Nine. Ten."

Another person's shadow approached the window. A man. They could see the silhouette of his tricorn hat and looming shoulders in a militia jacket.

"Eleven. Twelve. Fourteen."

Derick snickered. "Turtle always forgets thirteen."

Together, Molly and Archie recognized Becky's curly hair in the "soldier's" ponytail. Gasping, they exchanged a meaningful nod.

"Look at the window. That soldier wants to play hide-and-seek," Molly said.

"They can't play," said Archie loudly, loud enough to be heard all over the woods. "There's too many of them." Smart boy!

The windows were lit now, and the shadows of soldiers crossed back and forth in the light, lifting glasses, carrying plates. It was just Sybil and Becky and Mama, parading back and forth over and over again, making it look like the house was chock-full of militiamen having a party to celebrate leaving the parade ground.

Nothing could be further from the truth! After late March and early April spent drilling on the parade ground up the hill, Papa's regiment had gone home to

their planting. No more marching up and down. No wonder there were prowlers in the woods! They thought the Ludingtons had no protection.

Molly raised her voice. "Look at them all! They must have all got here at once."

"Fifteen, sixteen, seventeen," said Turtle.

"A whole regiment?" called Archie.

"There's too many of them to fit in the house!" Molly said. "They'll have to take turns at the food."

"Eighteennineteentwenty! Ready or not, here I come!" Turtle, oblivious to the activity inside the house, had his hands up comically, shading his eyes from the sides. He took a careful step into the yard.

"There's enough food," said Archie. "Mama's been cooking all day."

Not so. Mama had been huddled by the fire, taking care of her cold all day, hers and Abigail's, nursing the baby and drinking hot broth.

The back door opened, and Sybil stood there in an apron with something spilled down the front, her sleeves pushed up to her elbows and her shrew face on. Here came the shrew voice again, too. "Papa says if you rabble want any pie you'd better get in here! One. Two . . ."

Papa was not at the table. He was not even in the house. Papa was at the tavern in Fishkill with Mister Jay and General Washington, talking about getting muskets, bullets, and gunpowder for Papa's regiment from the stores at Danbury and White Plains.

The children crowded through the doorway.

"Stay away from the windows!" Sybil said. "Go right upstairs!"

"But I want pie!" said Turtle.

"Hush, there isn't any pie," Archie said.

They were halfway up the stairs when they heard the hooting. Were the bandits storming the house? A voice bellowed from beyond the yard, loud enough to penetrate right into the kitchen. "Ludington, come out, you coward!"

Sybil whipped open the back door and fired a shot into the black sky. The hooting stopped. Sybil stepped back in and smiled. "There's nothing but owls in the woods," she told the little boys.

Mama and Rebecca stood in front of the back window, each with her hair bunned up into a pigtail and tucked into the neck of a militia jacket, with some kind of padding underneath to make her shoulders bigger, and a tricorn hat low over her brow. Mama had a mug of ale in one hand and a plate in the other, Becky had just a plate and fork. They leaned toward each other and bobbed their shoulders against each other in the manner of men in a rowdy conversation. The effect of the shadows was convincing: the shadows were soldiers eating, drinking, having a celebration, filling up the house.

Sybil put on a pair of breeches she'd sewed for herself. She carried a musket and Papa's pipe. "Everybody go to bed, my spy heroes," Mama said to the children on the stairs.

"When's Papa due back?" asked Archie.

"A few more hours at least," said Sybil.

"One thing about all that hooting and hollering," Molly said. "He'll hear them before he gets close."

"And then he'll see the lights," added Archie. "What'll he do?"

"What do you think?"

"Hide out. Keep watch."

"Right," said Mama. "He'll see the shadows, too."

Sybil went outside and stood watch. Her musket on her shoulder, she circled from the back porch to the front, moving very slowly.

CHAPTER 10

In the wee hours after midnight, Papa returned from his meeting with General George Washington and Mister John Jay and found the house full of soldiers—or so it seemed, at first.

"I thought, what's this?" he said at breakfast. "The whole regiment is back! But then I realized there was some kind of spy show going on."

He was making light of it for the benefit of the little boys, Sybil thought, but he must surely have been worried, wondering who the spy show was being put on for.

He had stopped down the road as soon as he saw

the lights, tied Sir Kay, his horse, to a tree, and snuck up on foot to check out the house.

"I couldn't get close enough to see in the windows," said Papa. "I did see one soldier outside, on patrol. Quite thorough he was, too, circling the house—but not predictably, oh no! A little bit one way, a longer bit the next time, and now and then blasting a shot to the skies just in case anyone started thinking about stealing horses. Good man, Sybil."

Sybil was half-asleep at the table; she lifted her head from her arms, pushed Derick away from her last rasher of bacon with one hand, and raised the other to Papa in salute. Then she put her head back down. She raised it again briefly, when Papa brought out a gift Mister Jay had sent to the children. Molly's cry of delight was what made Sybil lift her head, but when she saw that the gift was a book of Greek myths, she dropped her head onto her arms again. The others crowded around Molly as she paged through the book—a grand volume, bound in green leather and including pictures of the strange and wonderful gods on Mount Olympus. "How could Mister Jay part with it?" asked Becky in wonder.

A typical gristmill. This one is located in Virginia.
[LC-USF33-011405-M3]

Papa shrugged. "He said he had already got a copy—courtesy of General Washington himself! We'll need to take especially good care of it; it's a treasure."

Sybil went out to the mill, sleepwalking but still running things. She and Molly had six bushels of buckwheat to mill for Sarah Hazen. Besides, a wagon was waiting at the gate. It wouldn't do to have customers pass the word that the Ludington mill was closed midday. Everything had to look normal, or tongues would wag. So Sybil dragged herself out, taking Molly with her.

On the bench of the wagon by the mill gate sat a tall lump of a boy with a white-blond pigtail, and a pretty pair of black horses with white diamonds on their foreheads. Fat flour sacks filled his cart. They bore the stamp of Red Mills. This man had come a long way to show off that he'd given his business to Beverly Robinson's gigantic mill. Not very polite.

Then Sybil recognized him as Peaceable Moon, the messenger who had brought Leazar's coded love note to Becky before Christmas. Several more love notes—real and pretend—had passed back and forth, courtesy of regimentals passing through Shaw's Pond toward the Hazens and the Carvers. The fact that the letters had all arrived at their destinations, without so far being intercepted or interpreted, was a good sign. So far.

"Sorry to trouble thee again, miss," Peaceable said. "I have a letter for Colonel Ludington." He slipped a thick square of paper out of his shirtsleeve.

"That's got *Sybil's* name on it," Molly said.

"I was asked to deliver it to Colonel Ludington. It's from Mistress Deborah Carver."

"No, it's a love letter to *her*," said Molly, pointing at her sister.

"From her son Timmy Carver," said Sybil, taking it.

"Miss Ludington?" A brown head popped up from between the gray grain sacks. "I'm here to tell you that your father's in danger," said a dark-skinned girl. She stood up and jumped from the back of the wagon. She was Sybil's height exactly, in a homespun gray gown spotted white with flour and speckled muddy at the hem.

The Quaker moved between the two girls as though to protect the brown girl behind his large self. "It's all right, Peaceable," she told him, pushing him gently aside.

"In danger? Who from?" Mama was in the doorway, one hand behind the doorjamb, surely gripping her musket.

"My master," said the girl. "Doctor Prosser. He's mustered a regiment. Fifty men, with more promising to come. He hasn't got the money to pay the men, only he promised he'd get it. He's stopping here to take your father along with him to General Howe."

At a sound from the porch, they all turned to see Papa there with Mama. "So those men last night were with Prosser. I'll see him horsewhipped, the damn'd—"

"He's already been here," Molly burst out. "And we saw him off without what he came for."

"Ha!" laughed Peaceable. "Poorer than he started!"

But the girl didn't laugh. She clasped her hands together in horror. "He'll have gone home, then, and he'll find me gone! He'll get me when he knows what I've done!"

Papa came down the steps and reached for her hand. "No, miss," he said. "If Prosser was leading those men, then he's gone to New York City. Word reached Colonel Morehouse this morning about the men in our woods. Morehouse surrounded them! He marched them off to jail two by two."

The girl pressed her lips together, her eyes gleaming. Peaceable clapped her on the shoulder with his ham of a hand, and she broke into a smile. She had dimples. "I'd never have waited if I thought they meant to come last night!"

Peaceable said, "The plan must have gotten moved up after thou heard it. Maybe Doctor Prosser got some new information."

Mama reached to shake the girl's hand. "Who are you that you took such a risk to come here and warn us of this?"

"A Patriot, ma'am," she said. "But I'm Hannah, Mistress Prosser's girl."

"A Daughter of Liberty," said Papa.

CHAPTER 11

"What made *you* decide to be a Patriot?" Mama asked Peaceable.

Peaceable shrugged. "I can offer no opinion on such things," he said, then added, "There were plenty of men up Pawling way who were ready to go with Prosser."

"Yes, but I wonder how many were willing to attack a family home," said Papa. "Surely that effort lost him some men. Prosser was a better man once." Peaceable glanced at Hannah, and she shrugged as if she didn't believe it.

"General Howe will get more men one way or the other," said Sybil.

"Well, they'll be quartered on us if he does," said

Peaceable. That sounded like a hint of an opinion to Sybil, so she gave a little whistle, which made him smile.

The Quakers didn't believe in warfare. The British generals, needing shelter for their troops all winter, had "quartered them" with families who were Loyalists, or neutral, like the Quakers were supposed to be. It meant they had to let the soldiers sleep in their houses and feed them as if they were guests.

Peaceable was risking the fury of more than just Doctor Prosser if it was known that he'd brought Hannah to warn the Ludingtons. Sybil tried to imagine what it was like not to be able to tell even your own family your opinions.

"Mister Jay sent me with a letter for Miss Sybil Ludington," Peaceable said. "Mistress Carver gave it to him."

"It's from Timmy," said Molly.

"Hannah," Sybil asked," how did you wind up in Peaceable's wagon?"

"He picked me up along the road," the girl said.

Sybil considered this: Mama wouldn't allow her daughters to be out on the road without a horse or cart. How much more dangerous was it for Hannah, alone, a dark girl without a horse?

"What were you doing on the road in the first place?"

"I wasn't *on the road*," Hannah said. "I hid in the trees until I saw the wagon."

It was wise of her to have picked Peaceable. More and more, he didn't seem like a typical Quaker.

"Who's Timmy?" Hannah wondered.

"Sybil's in love with him," Molly explained. Sybil bopped her on the head.

Becky glared at Molly, but Mama only blinked. So did Peaceable, politely pretending he hadn't heard. Hannah dimpled up again. Sybil opened the letter.

Its margin was doodled with 2s and hearts and initials, with a very simple message:

Dear Sybil, sweet, trust me, this letter's messenger carries my heart. Thanks, my love.

Timmy

---

* The 2s indicate that she should read every second word: Sybil, trust this messenger. My thanks. Love, Timmy

"Thank you," said Papa with a nod of gratitude to Peaceable.

"At your service," said Peaceable.

Hannah looked worried. "I can't go back there," she told Peaceable. "If they know I've come here, I don't know what they'll do to me."

"Then what *will* you do?" Becky asked.

The girl was at a loss. "I'd go north if I knew how," she said. "Quebec, I heard that's a place to go. But I don't know if that's right."

"It's true the French Canadians would be glad to deny British subjects their slaves," said Papa. "But they don't want anybody passing through from here to there. If the British in Canada come down the river to meet the British in New York, that's bad news for anybody in between—as well as us."

Hannah folded her hands and seemed to grow smaller. "I don't know what to do, then," she said.

"You can stay here for now," said Papa. "Prosser won't be back. It's the last place he'd come. He knows I've got my guns out for him."

"Besides," said Mama lightly, "I could use another hand around the place."

Sybil felt a little vibration go around the family as,

wordlessly, she and her sisters and parents made up their minds to trust Hannah.

"You'll get in trouble if you help me!" said Hannah, although hope filled her eyes.

Papa chuckled. "I couldn't be in more trouble if I tried," he said.

"And besides," said Sybil, "we're used to pretending with people." So Peaceable needn't think the Ludingtons had given all they knew away.

"We've got spy skills," piped up Molly.

Hannah said, "You must, if you managed to keep that wicked man from getting your papa."

They would have liked to tell her the story.

CHAPTER 12

Ever since Papa's men had gone off to plant their fields, he'd been figuring how to get them back on duty in the shortest time possible.

First, he would somehow get word that his regiment was needed.

He thought the British were most likely to come from the south, from New York City. So a messenger might reach the Hazens' house near Shaw's Pond. One Hazen boy—say, Moses—could dash on horseback to the Carvers' house. And one—say, Leazar—to the Ludingtons'—

That would let the southern part of the regiment know they had to muster.

Papa studied the map and reckoned he needed a messenger for the northern half of the county. He chose the Carvers to pass the message, because they were north and west. A love note from Sybil—passed along innocently by anyone going to Robinson's Red Mills over by Big Pond—could be delivered to Timmy. A practice run was required.

Sybil set out one day, wearing her boy's breeches and jacket, with her hair bunched up under an old straw hat so that only one ponytail hung down. Disguised as a boy, she would drive to the big mills, look for Mistress Carver, and give her the letter for Timmy.

If the letter got lost or confiscated and opened, the person who found it would just see some sweet words. (Molly snickered.) But Timmy would know how to read it, and he'd get word to the northern half of the regiment.

Sybil and Becky went through several sheets of Mama's scrap paper, cutting and scribbling, before they came up with a letter that would pass as something a girl would write to a boy and that would work as a secret message, too.

Sybil knew what it would mean if the British got as far as Peekskill. Then they might get control of the Hudson.

Dearest Timmy,
I called your name and trusted it
would echo west to you and every bell
chime amen! Will you meet me, Timmy
my dear? Rivers babble a tender
lullaby human hearts find sweet
to read so send me back your
own song and let me know your
heart. Your Sybil

(Howe's men will arrive by Hudson.)

Just before Sybil left, Papa said, "I now have messages from New York. The British are definitely on their way."

What Patriot would dare send a message from New York City, full of soldiers, through Westchester, the so-called neutral ground, rife with Loyalists?

"It came out of Long Island," said Papa. "Across Long Island Sound. Up here from there."

"I heard," said Hannah, and they all turned toward her, "the whole message depends on a woman in a house on the shore."

"How so?" asked Mama.

"She's got a code of her own that she writes with handkerchiefs she hangs from the wash. Someone sailing over from Long Island reads the message and knows where the danger lies—in Fairfield or Redding or Bethel or even New Milford."

Sybil had heard of those places, but she hadn't visited them and had never seen the sea—only the big, old Hudson.

"And if she hangs a black petticoat on the line, that's another message."

Molly laughed. "That's silly," she said.

Papa cocked an amused eyebrow at Sybil. Then he

reminded his girls and Hannah about Margaret Corbin at the battle of Fort Washington, where the poor, outnumbered Patriots only had two cannons, and the British were outgunning them severely. Margaret Corbin was at the battle with her husband, cooling the hot guns with water and helping load them, as many women did. Her husband was hit by a cannonball and fell mortally injured, right there beside her. "What did the good wife do?" asked Papa. "She grabbed the ramrod and the gunpowder and kept on going, firing that cannon into the devils—until she herself was taken down."

"Did *she* die?" asked Hannah.

"No, miss," said Papa. "They call her Captain Molly. How's that for a story?"

On the way to Robinson's mills, Sybil took Becky to call at Leazar's house. Becky would help Sarah Hazen with the dyeing she did for the regiment's wool and Sybil would pick up two big sacks of wool to take to the mill. It would be Sybil's excuse for going there.

The road was full of traffic. Dutchess County was smack in the middle between Hartford, Connecticut, and Fishkill, New York. People on all sorts of business passed through, from military to trade to farmers, fishermen, and trappers going to market, as well as those who hoped to make their living at the expense of such travelers.

It wasn't safe for girls, especially two whose father had a price on his head. Many was the farmer who brought in hired hands at planting time. People were more likely to assume there was a hired boy driving their cart—with a musket under the seat—than think that Colonel Henry Ludington had sent out his daughters on their own on some kind of a mission. But that was what he had done.

Only after Sybil had dropped Becky at the Hazens' did Hannah pop her head out from between the bags of wool and inform Sybil of her presence. Sybil nearly fell into a faint.

"What are you doing here? Why are you always hiding in carts?"

"Spying," said Hannah. "You might need me, so don't take me back."

Through gritted teeth, Sybil said, "How do you intend to help?"

"I'll do what I'm good at—hide in the cart. I'll

listen when you can't, and even when you can. And I'll be a second pair of hands if you need one."

"Hannah," said Sybil over her shoulder once they were on the road again and Hannah was tucked into the wagon bed among the wool, "if you give me away and break my trust, I will do the same to you."

There was a silence, then, "What makes you think I would do that?"

"What makes me think *anybody* would do *anything*? Maybe your own safety is more important than mine. Maybe your own secrets are more important to you."

Hannah said, her voice deep and quiet, "I am alone in this world, and your family took me in. I cannot say what I will and won't do, but I promise you—if I can help you make your way, I will."

Sybil, supported by her large family, felt humbled. What was it like to be always hiding? Outside the mills, she tied up in the shade of someone's barn and checked the letter in her breeches pocket. The letter was clearly addressed to Timothy Carver, Jr., but the return was just an *S*, with a flourish and daisies drawn in the loops. Sybil had sometimes written her initial to look like the snake on General Gadsden's flag, the yellow one that said DON'T TREAD ON ME, but she had never made it as girlish as this!

Robinson's Red Mills was a village of red-painted barns—the mills—built where streams from two big lakes channeled through stone-lined troughs. The waterwheels turned in these troughs, powering a mill for woolens, a grist mill for grains, and a sawmill for wood. It wasn't bustling like a market, with people chasing around on errands. Sybil guessed this was what *milling around* meant: everyone had to wait for the wheels to do their work. Men, women, children, servants, millers, and landowners wandered the spaces in a tense patience, talking to whatever acquaintances

An old water-powered gristmill with the wheel visible.
[LC-USF33-011410-M5]

they came across, catching up since the last time, which could have been hours ago or could have been months. No wonder people came here to get news.

Sent out to be a spy, to eavesdrop on conversations, read between lines, pick up clues, and solve mysteries, Sybil expected to have to do a little work. The last thing she expected was to hear a buzz of voices talking about the very thing she had come to find out.

"British ships have set sail going north."

"They're going upriver to Peekskill, carrying soldiers aplenty."

Who said that? At first Sybil saw nothing but the business faces of strangers from a part of the county she didn't get to much. Finally she identified the speakers: two well-to-do-looking men grumbling to themselves about the tenants of the Philipses.

"It's good news for our redcoated soldiers. Let the rabble starve!" said one, a bare-headed fellow with a ponytail, a clean blue waistcoat, and a dark brown boy to carry his sack of flour.

"As it should be. Justice will be served on these so-called Patriots. Whose manors are these crops grown on, after all? Not theirs!" said his friend, a round man with a tricorn hat and a powdered wig.

Sybil tried to move through the crowd invisibly, her own mask of pretend covering her real face. She was an errand boy, not a spy sponge trying to soak up intelligence or pass a secret message.

"Minutemen indeed. The rebels can't even keep a militia at Peekskill," a brown-haired woman in a worker's apron said.

"Here it comes, they'll be calling out the bumpkin troops again. Bumpkins in a pumpkin, rolling up lopsided!" That sounded like Mistress Carver, Timmy's mother. But it didn't look like her. This woman was wearing a white wig—the sort no farmer hereabouts could afford. Yet Sybil knew the voice well enough. And who was she talking to? A tall, blond, heavy man with a ponytail and a square-topped hat: Peaceable Moon. Sybil jolted aside to hide her face and pulled her straw hat lower.

"Who was it they got up there last time? Which troops?" the bewigged customer asked.

Mistress Carver-as-a-rich-woman stood right next to the millstone, hovering over the miller, making sure he was doing everything right. Sybil knew her type of customer!

"Colonel Henry Ludington's regiment," said

Peaceable. She couldn't believe he would say her father's name. "That's what I heard Doctor Prosser say," he added. Was he some kind of spy himself? Or did he just get information by pretending to have an opinion?

Sybil kept her head down and walked closer to the millstone. She found that between the grinding and the water and the wheel, some people couldn't make themselves heard without raising their voices.

"That Ludington better look to the angels." That was the miller himself.

"Once the British take Peekskill, Danbury will be next." Another customer.

"And what's right in between? Dutchess County, that's right," said Mistress Carver.

Sybil scooted behind a pillar.

Timmy's mother was a born actress. She went on: "We've got rid of the Indians. We've got the Quakers doing what we need, and Canada on our side, after that last piece of business the rebels attempted. It won't be long now."

"Any minute." That was the miller again.

"Seems so, if Tryon has his way!" Peaceable said.

Tryon! Most hated name! General Tryon was the

one who said Papa had betrayed him. Tryon was the one who put the bounty on Papa's head. What was he doing? How could she find out?

"So much for the 'minutemen'!" said the miller.

"So much for Henry Ludington," said Peaceable.

Sybil choked back a gasp. Who was this Peaceable Moon? And what was *peaceable* about him? She hustled out of the grist mill and stood shaking in the dirt yard.

If Papa wanted to know the mood at the mills, well, Sybil had learned it: the Tories were out for blood. If he wanted the news, she had that, too: the British were on the move, and they weren't wasting any time.

She needed to walk right up to Mistress Carver, deliver her letter, and get out.

For a moment, she stood in the open door of the sawmill. In the next, someone plowed right into her and nearly bowled her over. She found herself spun back out the door and pushed up against the wall, the wind knocked out of her. Hannah whispered, "Scold me. Tell me how stupid I am!"

"What? What are you doing?"

"Excuse me, sir! Pray excuse me! Let me help you, sir." And with her eyes, Hannah insisted on more.

"Silly fool!" Sybil hissed. "Why don't you get out of the way?"

"Please, sir," Hannah said. "I've found that *tool* you were looking for." She led Sybil away from the sawmill, and while she did it, she whispered in her ear, "Tool? Carver? Get it?"

"I found her myself!" Sybil whispered.

Hannah hissed, "Mistress Prosser is in there. I don't want to bump into *her*."

Mistress Prosser? The wife of the hooting, howling wolf who would have invaded the Ludingtons' house to take Papa's head? Sybil would have liked to push her under the mill wheel.

"How did you avoid her?" she asked Hannah. Sybil glanced around as if expecting some evil-looking witch of a person to turn up at any second. Now it occurred to her that Peaceable had mentioned Doctor Prosser. Was it some kind of warning to her or Mistress Carver?

Suddenly Hannah spun away and sped toward the door. "Small blond woman," Hannah said, and dove out of sight behind the building.

Sybil took a breath. "Help you carry your goods, ma'am?" She presented herself to the small blond woman, who immediately dumped a basket of linens into her arms and marched on. She was dainty, wearing her hair done up as if it were wigged.

Sybil-the-boy traipsed behind her, lugging the pile. In horror, she saw Mistress Carver and Peaceable Moon ahead, about to cross her path. She ducked her head and hid her face among the linens as Mistress Prosser paused. Mistress Carver went sweeping past, but Peaceable stopped as though he had been waiting for Mistress Prosser—and maybe he had.

"Where have you been, dear Mister Moon?" Mistress Prosser dropped her voice. "And what have you learned?"

"Only what we already know, ma'am. Doctor Prosser and his men have been taken by the Patriot rebels, and the British are moving up the river." Rebels! Sybil wanted to drop the linens and run. Peaceable seemed to be on both sides at once! Or, could he be saying the words Mistress Prosser would want to hear?

"Well, they can't get here a minute too soon," Mistress Prosser said. Her voice was soft and sweet. "They'll take what's rightfully theirs, and they'll open that jail in Fishkill if they know what's good for them. And Danbury, too."

"Have the redcoats come to Danbury, ma'am?" asked Sybil, keeping her voice low and gruff, keeping her face tilted away from Peaceable.

"Not as far as I know," said Mistress Prosser. "They're frightfully slow. Get a move on, then, Moon. Take that basket."

Sybil thrust it at him and turned away. Mistress Carver came walking purposefully toward her. "Young man, *you're* in the wrong place. I asked you to meet me in woolens, not linens. Poor lad doesn't know his linsey from his woolsey!"

Peaceable looked right into Sybil's eyes, but he said nothing, and she couldn't help it if he knew her now. Mistress Carver hustled her away into a street of shops. She was a few steps ahead when Hannah came flying up and said low in Sybil's ear, "Six ships sailed up to

Compo, in Connecticut. It's twenty miles from Danbury." She dashed away.

Mistress Carver turned, her eyes on Hannah's retreating back. "Who was that?" she asked.

"A friend," said Sybil. She pushed her letter into Mistress Carver's hand.

"Go right home," Mistress Carver said. "Godspeed." She herself stood rooted to the spot, holding the love letter as if it were a treasure. "Timmy will be overjoyed to get this letter."

Did she think the love letters were real? Sybil wanted to weep. She wanted nothing more than to come clean and say, *Mistress Carver, that letter is just pretend.*

Why hadn't Mama and Papa told her Mistress Carver wasn't in on the secret that she and Timmy weren't really in love? Sybil turned and walked away.

She was back in the cart, hurriedly shaking the reins at Lady Jane, when Hannah sprang into the back and hid herself, light and quick. She stayed hidden until after they left the Hazens', even as Becky and Leazar came laughing out the door to try to pull Sybil in for supper. Sun peeked through the clouds at the buds on the lilac bushes in the Hazens' yard. Raindrops spattered down over the doorway, making multicolored light.

"I want to make it home before the rain gets any harder," Sybil called across the yard.

"Come on, Sybil! You act like you're made of sugar," teased Becky.

"Just like her sister," said swoony Leazar. He walked Becky to the wagon and boosted her into the seat, his hands on her waist.

Sybil glanced away, then back again. "Leazar," she said, "the British have landed in Connecticut—twenty miles off—and they are marching north. We have to be ready for the muster."

Oh, how the light went out of their faces.

"Tell Mose," Sybil said. She meant Leazar's brother, Moses, three years younger.

"And my mother," said Leazar. He looked like his heart might weigh him to the ground.

Becky jumped back down and threw her arms around him. She held the back of his shiny brown hair in her hands and kissed him on the mouth. Sybil couldn't look away. Nobody was at the door or in the yard. It was just the four of them (Hannah peeking through a gap in the boards).

Then Leazar reached up and squeezed Sybil's arm. She dropped her hand onto his head and pushed it away.

Becky leapt back into the wagon. Sybil touched Lady Jane on the back, and they rolled away. Tears coursed down Becky's cheeks.

At last she asked, "How far is twenty miles?"

"It's a day's march," said Sybil. "If nobody tries to stop the redcoats. But somebody'll try to stop them."

"Who?"

"Connecticut has Patriots, too," Sybil said.

"So, one day to Danbury. Another day to us."

"We'll stop them if nobody else does," said Sybil boldly.

"And another day to Peekskill. Then what'll happen?"

Sybil was silent. She drove on, her shoulders hunched against the rain, which was getting heavier and chillier as the day darkened toward night.

"Mistress Prosser will be glad," Hannah said, sitting up.

"What are you doing here?" asked Becky.

Sybil and Hannah told her what they had learned at the mill.

"That's absurd," said Becky when they'd finished.

"What is?" Sybil wasn't sure which part her sister found most absurd—that Hannah had been there? That the British were coming? That Mistress Carver thought the love letters were real?

But this long day wasn't over yet. As they neared Shaw's Pond, a figure at the side of the road held up a hand. "Solomon Hopkins!" said Becky. Hannah slid down into the wool.

"The Misses Ludington," the man said—as if Sybil weren't even disguised as a boy. She sat silently, the reins in her hands, and waited for what came next.

"Can we help you, Mister Hopkins?" asked Becky.

"If there are no regimentals at your house tonight, stand the big drum on its end."

Becky's eyes were huge. "Yes, sir," she said. She nudged Sybil. Sybil drove on.

CHAPTER 13

Enoch slipped in the back door and stood thawing out, rubbing his hands together. "Winter's not quite letting go!" he said cheerfully. After that he was all business—"family business"—he said, looking around sternly at the Ludington children to be sure they'd keep his visit secret.

They smacked their hands on the table, which was spread with a map of the county and a basket of clay marbles, to represent the houses where members of the regiment lived.

There were 392 members in all, and they would all need to be on their toes if the redcoats used Connecticut as a path to the Hudson. Which way were the

redcoats marching? To Danbury? To Peekskill? By
what route? And what would they be doing along the
way? Battling whole towns? Ferreting out Patriots?
Taking prisoners? Taking young boys who might grow
into soldiers in time to fight?

"What's your plan?" Enoch asked Papa.

"Ain't no plan," said Colonel Henry Ludington
gloomily. "Not one that doesn't involve half the regiment riding like the devil to call out the other half!"

Enoch did a mental calculation. "That would mean
two hundred, give or take a few. And the British have"—
he glanced at Papa to see what he knew, but Papa just
waited apprehensively—"two thousand, Colonel."

"We'll need every man," Papa said staunchly.

"You'll need *me*," insisted Sybil.

"And me," said Rebecca with less conviction.

"There *are* some girls suiting up as militiamen,"
said Enoch gently, with a little smile just for Sybil.

"Over my cold, dead, rotting body," Papa said.

"But they're your right-hand men," Archie reminded
him.

"They're women," said Papa.

Sybil crossed her arms over her chest and held her
chin high. "Then we'll ride to call out the regiment."

"And me," Molly said, jumping up.

"And me, too," said Archie. They all stood just like Sybil, shoulder to shoulder.

Enoch went and put his arm around Mama, who had Abigail in her arm, lower lip between her teeth.

"Children," said Papa. "You make me proud. General George Washington would say—"

They never found out what the general would say. They found out what Mama would say. "You will not," she said. "There will be men coming down this road in both directions, and the house must be defended. I can't do it alone. I'll need one of you big girls in here with me at all times, and one outdoors on watch."

"We'll make a plan," said Papa tensely. "After that we'll see who will execute it. Let's plan the alarm first. We need to find the shortest route that will take us to every house in the county."

Together they pored over the regiment roster, placing marbles along the roads and paths and byways of the county, one for each household that would need to be called out. Then Becky used scraps of charcoal to begin marking a series of trails designed to take a rider— or riders—most efficiently and quickly from one house to another.

Everyone disagreed about which route would be shortest and fastest. The map became a spiderweb maze of routes, each failed or flawed in length or direction. One was too long. One involved too much back and forth. One went straight through what used to be Indian country and was still populated with squatters and ne'er-do-wells.

"Wait!" Molly said. She grabbed Becky's pen and ink, drew circles around the marbles set on the map, and removed them one by one. Everybody stood around and grumbled, but nobody stopped her.

When she was done drawing, she swept the map off the table and carried it into the weaving room. "Bring some light!" she called back with authority, so they did. Rebecca and Sybil each followed with a lantern and stood on either side of Molly, lighting the wall as she took the big warping frame from its two hooks, stuck the map up there instead, and rehung the frame.

Enoch and Papa scratched their heads, but when Becky tied the end of a string onto the peg nearest the ink circle marked HOME, the light dawned. Together they conferred about which house should be next, and Molly led the string to the peg nearest that house. On and on they went, until they reached the last house and tied the string off.

Then another string was tried. The girls' hands flew around, seeking a shorter route. In the end, the string wound past—or within earshot of—each house in the regiment. The route that took the shortest length of string, followed actual roads, and didn't cross water (except over bridges) was the winner.

"Maybe if you have a problem you should ask a girl," Molly said, but the result was just more argument about who would ride the wonderful route.

Should Papa ride and Sybil stay home?

"No," said Mama. "You'll be too tired, then, Henry, and you'll still have to lead the regiment to God knows what disaster. No one else can ride as fast as you, besides Sybil."

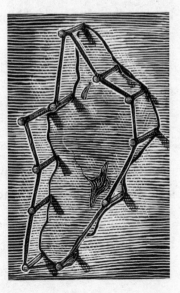

Each person—Sybil, Moses Hazen, Deborah Carver, and Becky— would ride from home when the alarm came in.

Papa would stay here, on guard, waiting for his men to arrive and getting things organized when they did. Mama would have an enormous pile of food, and the little boys and Archie and Molly would serve it and run errands and anything else that needed doing.

"Enoch, where will you be?" Sybil asked.

There was a lot of throat clearing before she divined the answer: gone, turned invisible, off on his own adventure, away doing secret things.

Sybil glowered openly at Enoch and was satisfied to see his gray eyes turn down, his head cocked to one side regretfully.

She continued to stare him down: *tell me.* Then, in her ear, he whispered, "North."

"Where?"

"Where the British will be going next if they reach the river."

"Canada?"

Sybil met Hannah's questioning eyes across the room.

"You're going to Canada?" Hannah asked Enoch softly. "They haven't got slaves there, have they?"

"Not as many as here," said Enoch. "But slaves heading there get taken for spies, sometimes."

"Then where can one go to be free?"

Sybil felt her own eyes tear up. With all this talk of freedom around here, it was awful that Hannah needed to go elsewhere. But where?

Enoch said quietly, "Vermont will vote on abolishing slavery this very summer. That's the place I'd go if I wanted to be among sympathetic folk."

Hannah nodded. Enoch exchanged a glance with Sybil, and she nodded, too.

The group's attention was caught by the sound of hooves coming up the road from Shaw's Pond. Papa went to the door and talked quietly to the man on the horse. The rest of them stood waiting in the hall. The brook was loud as a river, full with spring. Peeper frogs were screeching along its banks and in the timberland. The natural world—of rivers and frogs and skunks, owls and opossums, seed corn and new peas—was going on as if it hadn't heard the reports of war on the way.

Papa's voice rose. "Thanks, friend!" The horse went drumming away down the hill. Papa returned to his chair at the head of the table. The family came and sat, too. Enoch stood behind Sybil's chair. She leaned against its back as though she'd have liked to lean on him.

"Henry," said Mama. Meaning, *tell*.

"Seventeen gallant Patriots confronted the troops

north of Compo Beach as they tried to cross the Post Road."

"Hooray!" said Hank. Then he saw the solemnity on the rest of the faces, and shrugged. Derick shrugged, too, and Turtle tried to.

Papa continued, "There were far too few of them to make much trouble, and they were dispersed with gunshots and the threat of bayonets. A few British soldiers were wounded or killed. They were carted back to the ship. The rest marched on through a place called Aspetuck, and they're camped along the river there for the night."

"What do they have to do to get here from there?" Molly asked. "Is Aspetuck on our map?"

"No," said Enoch. "It's too far away to be on our map. And the soldiers are bedded down for the night." But the worry on the elders' faces was clear, and the children grew anxious, too.

"Come, boys," said Mama. "You too, Archie. Bed."

Archie scowled. Molly gave him a little smile as if to say, *I'll find out what I can.*

"Papa," she said when they'd gone up, "are Continental soldiers going to try to get the redcoats while they sleep?"

He shook his head. "General Benedict Arnold is called in from New Haven, along with General David Wooster. Their troops will meet General Gold Selleck Silliman on his way from Fairfield."

Her jaw dropped. "And they need our regiment, too?"

"Not yet, Molly. But if they come this way . . ." Papa hesitated, then gave her the hard facts. "The British have five times as many troops as our regiment. And every one of them has a rifle and bayonet, good boots and a helmet."

Papa's soldiers didn't have a single helmet among them.

"The question is," said Papa to Enoch, "how are we going to find out what happens next?"

One possibility came from an unexpected quarter. Hannah said, "I haven't seen Peaceable Moon come back from Big Pond yet. I've been watching. He would have to go the long way around to avoid passing this house."

Sybil pictured the long road she and Hannah and Becky had traveled back from the mills this afternoon. Peaceable could have passed her and Hannah when they turned off to the Hazens, but only if he had been close behind them.

"He could have stayed in Big Pond," Sybil mused.

"What friend would a young Quaker have to stay with thereabouts?" asked Mama.

"He could have camped along the way," said Enoch.

"Being out in the night with horses might draw Cow Boys or Skinners," said Sybil.

Benedict Arnold (1741–1801), a general in the Continental Army, eventually defected to the British Army.
[LC-USZ62-68483]

"And aren't Quakers supposed to be peaceable and not carry firearms?" asked Becky.

Hannah heard them out, then said—her eyes on Papa, who hadn't spoken—"Peaceable has some secret places."

"Can he be trusted, then?" asked Papa.

"He knows more than people think," said Hannah. Sybil thought this was true of Hannah, as well.

Papa leaned in and said more forcefully, "Can he be trusted?"

Hannah sighed. "Some say he can."

"What does that mean?"

"Colonel," said Enoch in a soothing voice, "a Quaker has certain loyalties—to his family and to his faith."

"Is he a Patriot or not?" said Papa.

"That remains to be seen," said Mama.

With Enoch bedded down by the fire for the night, the Ludingtons went up to bed, although not all slept well; their minds were too full of possibilities.

Sybil lay awake, listening to Becky snore and wondering what Hannah—sharing Molly's bed—was thinking. When she had nearly dozed off, she heard footsteps creep out of the room and down the stairs, and voices from below—Hannah consulting with Enoch, fugitive to fugitive.

Sybil tiptoed to the top of the stairs and sat there in her nightgown, waiting. The back door opened softly, then closed again, followed by an odd sound—something rolling back and forth in a little motion. It was the drum, laid on its side again. Enoch must have moved it as he left.

Sybil stood, intending to go to the window to try to catch a glimpse of him, but just then Hannah came padding softly up the stairs, not noticing Sybil until she was nearly at the top. Wearing one of Mama's nightgowns, which swallowed her up, she sat down on the step. She folded her hands around her knees and whispered, "Do you think I can walk a hundred miles? That's how far it is just to the border of Vermont."

Sybil sat next to her and said, "You could just stay. Papa won't let the Prossers have you."

Hannah gave a little smile of thanks, and sighed. "What's that thing you all say? Family secret?" She patted her knee.

"Family business!" said Sybil.

"Oh yes!" They both patted their hands on their knees.

Hannah leaned her cheek on Sybil's shoulder, then stood and went to bed. Sybil climbed in beside Becky, and for a moment, she and Hannah looked across and caught each other's eye in the starlight. Then they slept.

CHAPTER 14

Peaceable Moon arrived early the next morning, having spent the night (he said) near Robinson's mills. As he passed through Shaw's Pond, just after dawn, he'd been stopped by Solomon Hopkins, who asked him to carry a basket of morels and fiddlehead ferns and dandelion greens to his dear friend Abigail Ludington.

Hannah held the horses while Peaceable took the basket inside. Sybil thought that was strange: Why hadn't Peaceable just handed the basket to Hannah?

"Treasure!" said Papa at the sight of the morels. "How are things with Solomon?"

Peaceable smiled. "He said, 'Tell Abigail that morels and scrambled eggs make a feast for the gods.'"

"Well, Solomon is a dear friend," Mama told Peaceable. Sybil thought that was an exaggeration. "Let me
make you up a parcel of morels to take home to your
family, Mister Moon." Mama took the basket into the
larder and emerged with a bundle of morels in a length
of linen toweling.

Peaceable wouldn't stay to breakfast. He took two
warm biscuits and headed outside. "My Star and Moon
need to get home to their hay beds," he said to Hannah.

Quite suddenly Hannah threw her arms around him
and whispered something Sybil couldn't hear.

Peaceable climbed up behind his black horses and
pressed off east toward Quaker Hill. In the kitchen,
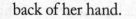Hannah dabbed at her eye with the
back of her hand.

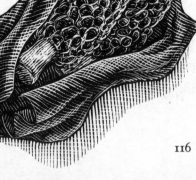"What?" said Han-
nah, seeing the sisters
stare.

"You're sad he's
gone?" asked Molly.

"He helped me get

away from the Prossers," Hannah said quietly. "I'd be indebted to the devil himself if he did that for me."

"There!" said Mama's voice from the larder. She emerged into the daylight of the kitchen with a small cylinder of paper in her hand. "Feast for the gods, indeed! Molly, fetch the book of Greek myths."

Solomon Hopkins had slipped the tiny rolled-up note into the bottom of the basket of morels, woven into the strands that formed the basket.

Becky gasped. "Why didn't he tell Peaceable it was there?"

"Maybe he didn't want to trust Peaceable," said Mama.

When Molly returned with the beautiful book, Papa had Solomon's paper unscrolled. Sybil couldn't tell anything from it. Instead of words, it had numbers all over it, written in rows the way words normally were.

112. 139. 217. 453. 323.
627. 93. 481. 165. 97. 24.
590. 11. 376. 86. 221. 7.

"Now then, Captain Molly," Papa said gently. "Page 112."

Molly set the book on the table, thumbed through to 112, and spread the pages under a careful hand. "It's the story of Apollo," she said. "The sun god riding on his chariot across the sky."

"What's the word?" asked Papa. "The underlined word?"

The girls pored over the book. Becky skimmed the page and found it. *"Sunrise,"* she said.

"Now, 139."

"Icarus flying too close to the sun," Sybil said. *"Burning."*

"217?"

"Houses."

"453?"

"It's just a big letter *R*."

"Maybe that's for Redding or Ridgefield," said Papa. "Next is 323."

"E," Becky said. "Redding."

Observant Archie asked, "They are burning houses in Redding? Where's Redding?"

"Not far," said Papa. "They are on their way north to Danbury."

Sybil could spare little thought for the massive surprise of learning that the Greek myths book—the one Mister Jay could spare because he had one of his own from General Washington—held the key to a code used to send a message through Peaceable.

The British had marched to Redding, Connecticut, before most civilized people had breakfast. They were looking for rebels and trying to kill boys in their families old enough to become soldiers who might fight them. A Patriot on a hilltop in Bethel had managed to trick the British into thinking that great

A depiction of the Battle of Bunker Hill in Massachusetts, 1775.
[LC-DIG-pga-00085]

regiments of soldiers awaited them. They were held up for two hours waiting for the attack before moving on. The message ended with the British marching north to Danbury. General Arnold was headed there to confront them.

"When the devil is he getting there, I'd like to know," Papa burst out. He paced the room. "Where are they going after that, Abby?" he asked Mama. "What's he after, that rascal Tryon, Sybil? Who's he meeting at Peekskill? Is Howe coming north, Becky? What's Jay doing over in Fishkill, Captain Molly?"

They all sat there gaping. Mama set the baby on the floor to sit among the boys and their toys. She put her arms around Papa. He wasn't really asking them anything, just trying to sort through the entire story in his mind as if it were a map with sections all unexplored. "Be ready," Papa said.

"We will be," Mama answered.

Papa went out. He checked on the horses in the paddock and the oxen and cows in the pasture, the seeds and weeds in the field, everything springing up now that it was the growing season. From the back window, they could see him walking, pacing, listening, thinking. With four hours to sundown, he harnessed up Chess and Checkers, hitched them to the plow, and carried on with the plowing. He must have wanted to go, go, go, but a soldier needed to wait for his orders.

"Leave him alone," Mama said to Sybil.

So Sybil sat on the back steps next to the lying-down drum and thought about information. She imagined secret trails, an almost invisible path made up of people: Solomon Hopkins, Peaceable Moon, and Hannah Prosser. And Papa.

When Sybil thought of what lay ahead, she knew one thing for sure: the regiment was going to be mustered together here. The plan included Becky and Moses and Mistress Carver and a chain of alarm—maybe clanging bells, or honking conch shells or clattering pots and pans.

She knew she could make the ride faster alone.

If she did, Moses could go along and help Leazar— one more man for the battle. Becky could stay on watch for Mama.

With her right finger, Sybil drew the letter *R* on her chest. *R* for *resolution*. *R* for *revolution*. She would ride the whole route herself or die trying.

Inside the house, the family cooked the way they did when a storm was on the way. Mama set extra bread to rise, and Becky kneaded the risen dough, divided it into rounds, and covered them up again. The boys were kept busy fetching and carrying from the cellar: dried beef, onions, potatoes, carrots, turnips, and the absolute barrel bottom of the apples. Becky made pies from the mince preserved in December. Three pots of stew simmered over the fire. The men of the regiment would be there soon enough, devouring it all.

Mama brought in the washing she had hung out that morning, dry now in the longest stretch of sun they'd had all week, and Molly ironed and folded.

Hank said, "What are we doing so much housework for?"

"To be ready," Molly said, but she didn't really know the answer. What was the answer? It felt good to be busy. None of them had any idea what they would be called upon to do tomorrow.

In a way it was a proud feeling. In a way it was very, very frightening.

As evening came on, they continued working. While Papa stayed out in the field, Sybil helped with the

milking, then came into the house. "I could get used to wearing these breeches," she told Mama.

Mama shook her head. "A girl needs to become a woman, not a man," she said.

Sybil rolled her eyes. "I could lead a regiment."

"Thank goodness you won't," said Mama.

Sybil thought a moment, but only said, "The rain's beginning again."

Mama smiled. "What a spring!"

It was just a drizzle, but it made the night come faster, so it made Papa retire sooner from the field. When he came in, the table was set with stew and fresh bread. All seemed strangely well, on the surface of things. The fire glowed in the hearth, and the room was still warm from the sunny day. Everything seemed clean and orderly. Even the boys had had their Saturday baths and sat shining and ready for bed.

But Hannah wasn't there.

It seemed like they all knew at once that she was gone. Sybil bolted up from her chair and headed for the door. Somehow, in the last light of day, she glimpsed a movement in the distance across the fields and chased after her, the breeches letting her run fast. At first

Hannah ran, too, and then she slowed and walked back toward Sybil. "What?" she said flatly.

"Vermont?" said Sybil. "Or off to tell Prosser our plans?"

Hannah's face showed her how wrong she was. "Family business," Hannah said fiercely. "I said it, and I meant it!"

"How do you know the way?" asked Sybil.

Hannah looked at her and waited.

"Enoch?" Sybil guessed.

Hannah nodded.

"Then you'll be safe," said Sybil. "I wish it was me!"

Hannah laughed.

Sybil pulled out the Daughter of Liberty medal that Molly had made and pressed it into Hannah's hand. "Don't let anybody see this until you know you're safe," she said. She turned on her heel and walked back toward the house.

"Don't forget me," called Hannah.

"Don't you forget me!" said Sybil.

Around the table, her family sat waiting, eating. She pulled her chair up and tucked into her supper and found herself unable to speak a word.

Mama spoke up. "She's got food and warm things," she said. "I saw to that." As the idea sank in that Hannah was gone, off on a long and dangerous journey, lightning flashed and thunder came rolling across the night sky. The rain came down in giant splats, then settled into a steady downpour.

Becky took the little boys to bed, and when she came back downstairs, she stood before Mama and Papa and said, "We have to talk about the plan." She wanted to go to Leazar's mother. "If the regiment is called out, she'll be there alone. Either I want to bring her here, or I want to go there. She's going to be my mother-in-law someday. I can't have her left sitting alone through some long battle, waiting to hear the worst kind of news. If something happens to Leazar or Moses or the others, I want to be there with her."

"Oh, my dear," said Mama. "That is kind."

"Who's going to take your leg of the route?" Molly asked, sounding hopeful and fearful all at once.

"Solomon might go stay with Mistress Hazen," said Papa. "There's no need for you to go, and your mother may need you here."

"I've been thinking, too," said Sybil. "If Becky took Kay, he'd be tired just when Papa needs him fresh. Better to take just Lady Jane the whole way around."

"You take the first part and let Deb Carver take the rest," said Papa.

"But that leaves me at the Carvers, and leaves Mistress Carver here," said Sybil.

"Listen," said Mama. She stood and went to the door, her face turned to the northeast and the road from Danbury.

Then came the hooves, fast and loud and nearing. Out of the gloom, a white-faced, storm-soaked man charged toward the door. "Henry Ludington! Colonel Ludington!"

CHAPTER 15

THE NIGHT OF
APRIL 26, 1777

———— *Nine o'clock* ————

"Message for Colonel Ludington from Colonel Cooke!" the man said, his chest heaving.

"Tell me what you know," said Papa.

The man inhaled to calm himself, then shifted his shoulders back so he seemed more official. "Danbury is burning, sir! Your regiment is wanted."

Papa stepped past Mama and Abigail. He grabbed the messenger's reins and gripped the man's arm to steady him as he slid to the step. Archie took his wet coat and offered him a shawl. Mama put a bowl of stew in his hand. All the while, he talked to Papa. The

British were taking things from barns and bringing them into the middle of Main Street to burn them. They were marking the houses of Loyalists, which made it seem like they were going to do something about the unmarked houses. Patriots who tried to defend the stores were being beaten and shot.

Abruptly Papa turned away. "Stay only long enough to water your horse," said Papa. "I'll get him under cover for you."

After the messenger finished his stew and ale, he went to look for Papa.

In the yard, he saw Sybil standing ready beside Lady Jane. "A girl, sir?" he called.

Papa tucked his lips in around his teeth, and his Adam's apple moved in his throat.

"Indeed, son. Sometimes a girl is the best man for the job."

He laced his hands together. Sybil stepped into his palms, and he boosted her up. Molly brought Sybil a strong branch, and with a final word of advice from Papa, Sybil gathered her reins. Then she was gone, with a clatter of Lady Jane's hooves through the muddy puddles, and away.

Out of sight around the bend, a figure darted

toward Sybil, and she pulled up to avoid running the fool over. "Becky!" Sybil gasped.

Her sister grabbed her hand. "Take me to Leazar's," she said.

"But Papa—"

"I don't care!"

There wasn't time to argue. Sybil pulled her sister up behind her.

———————— *Ten o'clock* ————————

Rain pelted down, wetting Becky's cloak, which she had wrapped around her back and Sybil's front, and which was only keeping about half the rain out. Rain dripped off the brim of Sybil's hood down her face and into her mouth. She blew it aside and peered into the deep, wet darkness.

"Are you still furious I'm here?" asked Becky.

"No, I'm glad," said Sybil. It was a lie and they both knew it, but there wasn't anything to be done.

"Are you going to marry him, then?" asked Sybil presently.

"If only I can," said Becky. "I love him like anything, Sybil. I can only wish the same happiness for you."

Sybil snorted. "Maybe Timmy Carver and I will find the same happiness," she said. Becky made her feel sarcastic, as if something vital in life had passed Sybil by.

"Aw, don't make fun of Timmy," scolded Becky. "He's got a true heart. You should live to deserve him."

That wasn't kind. "May he live to deserve me," said Sybil. "How fast do you think his mother can ride, anyway?"

She felt Becky shrug. "Mama said she used to beat all the boys. Like you."

"Well, I'd have liked to race her," said Sybil. "Maybe before she had two big sons."

Since Becky had begged off her leg of the route, Sybil knew she should have been more willing to let Mistress Carver take the northern half. Instead, she decided more firmly on a different plan. "I'm going to do the whole thing," Sybil said. "As soon as I get you off the back of this horse, that is."

Lady Jane cantered along, the girls moving with her. Becky leaned her head on Sybil's shoulder. "Why didn't you bring a musket?"

"Too much to carry. Too dangerous if someone wants to use it against me. Too few muskets, anyway."

Becky said, "But what if someone—"

"Who?"

"You know what I mean. A girl in the dark in the night alone . . ."

"You've got too much of an imagination, Becky."

"You haven't got enough, Syb."

"Yes, I do." Her voice told Becky exactly how far Sybil's imagination had gone.

"Oh, Syb."

"Oh, Beck."

"What if Leazar—"

"He won't."

"Syb, I love him so much. I'm going to be his wife when all this is done."

"I believe it."

Far below in the valley, lights still lit the windows in the village and reflected in Shaw's Pond. Just the long woods and marsh of Horse Pound Road lay in between. Sybil tugged the short reins attached to Lady Jane's halter and turned her to the right.

———— *Eleven o'clock* ————

"Yes, this is the alarm," said Sybil to Solomon Hopkins. "But you don't need to try to ride. Don't worry,

Mister Hopkins. Look, Becky's with me, and we'll cover the route to the Carvers'." She didn't tell him Becky was getting off within five miles.

He hesitated a minute but didn't try to deter her. "Hurry on to Big Pond now before it gets too late," he said. "I'll alert everyone hereabouts. Trust me."

Becky dared to tell him, "The morels were a feast for the gods."

He raised two fingers to his brow and gave a salute. "Go now," he ordered.

Sybil and Becky weren't a mile past his door, just coming onto Philip Smith's, Sybil's stick poised to knock, her throat cleared to shout, when the church bell began bonging. Solomon Hopkins himself must have been riding its rope, old war wound and all.

The doors opened before they reached them. The bell's note crossed the valley, echoed across the lake, and rattled the windows of the farmhouses on the far side.

In her chest, Sybil could feel the clapper strike the bell as she rode past Enoch's parents' farm. Best not to be seen stopping *there* on such a night, when everyone was out in the road to see what the matter was. On they rode, past the Merricks' (in the regiment) and the

Hamblins' (wide-awake, but not in the regiment) and on toward the Hazens'.

Sybil slowed a mile before Belden's Bridge, just long enough to let Becky slide off at the edge of the road—holding her wrist with one hand, letting go only when her sister's toes touched down. "Kiss him for me!" she said.

"I will," called Becky as she ran to the Hazens'.

Sybil would have liked to say Godspeed or to cross her heart, but there was no time to stop, and no sense in taking a hand off the reins longer than the time it took to wave good-bye. So she whispered a prayer that was more like a caution to God not to let another Hazen man be taken this spring, and rode on.

—————— *Nearly midnight* ——————

Just northeast of the town by Big Pond, Captain John Crane ran a tavern. You didn't need a signpost to point toward it; there were drunk idiots along the road over a three-mile radius. The drunker the better—they didn't notice a rider bearing down until she was nearly upon them. Was it better to be a girl or a boy? After one large, slack-jawed person grabbed at her skirt and

had to be repelled by a smack with the stick, Sybil stood in the saddle and wound the sodden skirt around her middle. Now she resembled nothing so much—when passing quickly on horseback—as a long-legged boy with an extra-thick middle. Good. Only when she'd safely passed these fellows did she dare to shout behind her, "The British are burning Danbury! Muster at Ludington's!"

At the tavern itself, she paused, jittery, sure the

revels inside would drown out her voice and not wanting to dismount.

The tavern had a yard, emptied now in the rain, that kept her from riding straight up to the door to knock with her stick. As the horse stood, as Sybil tried to decide, her hands flipped up unconsciously to twist her flopping hair back into its braid. She tucked it into the neck of her coat, put on the tricorn hat, and nickered to Jane, turning her away from the door, unable to decide.

Suddenly the door flung open and four merry farmers came slouching out. She didn't know them all, but Leazar's uncle, his mother's brother, a captain in the Seventh, was among them. Happy louts, with their arms around one another's shoulders, singing:

> *"Father and I went down to camp,*
> *Along with Captain Gooding,*
> *And there we saw the men and boys*
> *As thick as hasty pudding.*
> *Yankee Doodle, keep it up,*
> *Yankee Doodle Dandy—"*

"Mister Hazen!" Sybil called. He looked up, bewildered. What was this boy doing here, at a tavern, in

A tavern in the late 1700s. *[National Maritime Museum, Greenwich, London, Caird Collection]*

the middle of a rainy night, shouting at him? "The British are burning Danbury. Muster at Ludington's!" She saw understanding dawn on a face that in this light she could see had once been as handsome as Leazar's. "Tell Captain Crane," she called. She didn't wait to see what happened next. She rode on.

CHAPTER 16

APRIL 27, 1777

—— *Twelve thirty in the morning* ——

The part of the route where Sybil was most likely to be killed, tarred and feathered, jailed, or worse—for a girl, lots could be worse—had been pushed to the back of Sybil's mind.

No, be honest, she told herself. The threat had been real to her ever since she and Papa had first listed the houses of the men, and she saw how many of the militia lived within spitting distance of Robinson's Red Mills. Now she paused as she neared the mills.

It seemed that wherever she looked, she saw a person walking. Men, of course. Women didn't go out alone in the middle of the night.

Sybil had never been in Red Mills or anywhere around Big Pond at night. She didn't know what so many men were doing out. Were they all coming from the taverns? How far past Belden's Bridge had the alarms reached?

If only she had paid closer attention to the direction the sounds had come from as she rode. Had the alarm spread only to Shaw's Pond and no farther? Had it rushed on ahead of her to pave her way? She didn't know.

What if the chain of alarm *had* traveled up here? That might explain the men along the paths, waiting for word or heading off to muster. Some here were part of Papa's Seventh Regiment, but others belonged to nearby regiments—and surely many would be going off to fight for the king.

Sybil mustn't let herself look like a messenger of any sort. There could be no air of rushing about her. She decided she had to look as if she hadn't come too far. She let her hair out of her collar and smoothed what she could of her bib and tucker. Was it really best to be a girl here?

The wretched rain grew lighter at last. Sybil paused under a pine to wring the rain from her hood and carelessly dropped her stick into a ditch, but she dared not dismount here. She urged Lady Jane to a trot. She had to look hurried enough—no girl without an emergency at home would be out in this weather at this hour—but she shouldn't look like a hawk screaming down from a treetop, even if that was how she felt.

"Hi, lass!" She heard a booming German accent as a Hessian soldier used the rudest way to address a woman.

Another man rode up on her other side. "Young lady," he said in a Dutchess County accent. Not British. A Tory, then, a Loyalist, on the same side as the Hessian. What did they want with her? Who did they think she was? Sybil nodded, touched her heels to her horse, and rode on. "Good night," she said.

"Too proud for the likes of us," said the Tory.

"Stay, miss!" said the Hessian.

Sybil kept her face forward, then nearly fell from her horse as another man grabbed at the reins. This one stood on the ground and must have merely reached out his hand as she'd worked at avoiding the horsemen. "Hey!" she exclaimed without thinking.

"Yes? On your way somewhere at such a late hour, miss?"

"Mistress Pinckney's," Sybil said. "My mother . . .

Please, sir. I need to get word to Mistress Pinckney about my mother." Her brain ran forward to the many, many houses of militiamen whom she had not yet called out, the regiment soldiers who did not know what was happening.

She willed this man away from her, while calling up the little drama she and Becky had practiced for just such a case as this. "To what purpose?" he asked.

Strange question, but they had planned for it.

"It's her milk," said Sybil. "Her left teat is blocked. It's red and it's making her life a misery. And"—here she put her face in her hands and sniffed loudly, and it was easy enough to pretend she was crying, since her face was still wet with rain—"the baby can't suck without causing pain, so they're both crying, and it's making the baby get a rash—"

The man snorted lightly.

Before he could start throwing his weight around, Sybil pounced. "Sir, you know this is a dangerous area for a girl. I'd be grateful for a messenger."

"Send a messenger where? Mistress—"

"Pinckney," she repeated. He didn't know who that was, so she just made up the directions and said, "Past the mill. Up the hill. Past the mill pond, then it's not the first house on the left, and it's not the second, but you'll see a huge sycamore tree, which takes eight people to stand around, and then there's a little brook coming down the right side, and just before you get to the—"

"Good Lord, girl."

She sighed like a dizzy twit. "I know. And in this weather! Well, I'm wet already, I'll just carry on." She reached for the reins and nickered to the horse, but the man held on to the reins.

At this, Sybil's heart banged in her chest. He wasn't going to let her go. He was going to pull her down and find her out and send her to General Gage and the prison ship. How could she reach for the knife in her pocket and keep her grip on the reins as well?

"You know," she said calmly. "What would make it ever so much safer would be to have an escort."

He stood there wavering.

"There and back, of course," said Sybil.

"Back?"

"Hamblins," she said. "A mile past Belden's Bridge." On purpose, she was asking far too much.

From up the road to one side, the side away from Big Pond, footsteps splashed and echoed, more men coming. The man inched one fist closer to her along the reins, grabbed her wrist in the other, and pulled her toward him.

"I'll scream," she said softly.

"Godspeed," he said solemnly, as if claiming her. He let her go, pushed her away, as a man carrying a musket neared them along the path.

Sybil kicked Jane and took off at a gallop.

——— *One o'clock in the morning* ———

Half a mile beyond the mills, Sybil reached a stretch of road with no people—no visible people, anyway. She jumped down and hunted for another long, thick stick. On Jane's back again, she needed only to thump the butt of her stick on the doors of the houses on her list.

Deborah Carver peeked through the crack of her door as Sybil came charging up. She had an expression like Mama wore when riders rode past: What now? What bad news was this?

"Muster at Ludington's!"

Mistress Carver, usually so quick to say something funny and gay, reached for Sybil's wrist and laid a soothing hand on Lady Jane's neck. "Where are they marching, Sybil?"

"To meet the British wherever they go next after Danbury."

Behind Mistress Carver the door opened wider. Timmy's father and his brother, Barnabas, were there. "These merry men!" said Deb, smiling affectionately. "Off on their bold adventure, like Robin Hood!" From horseback, Sybil could see over their heads into the room, where Timmy was bent by the hearth stuffing something into a knapsack. He looked serious enough, but his mother was trying to make light of matters.

"Half a moment, and I'll be ready to ride off like Maid Marian herself!" Mistress Carver went on.

"No, I'll ride on," said Sybil. "Mistress Carver, I know you meant to ride the rest of the way, but that would leave me here. So I'm just going to keep on going."

Deborah Carver seemed to cave in a little, then she rallied again. "So I'll stay here and protect the castle." She paused, downcast. "Stop for a bite, for a drink," she told Sybil, and saw in the girl's face that she couldn't stop for anything. It made Sybil's stomach clench to see wonderful Mistress Carver suddenly frightened.

"What about a fresh horse?" called Timmy to Sybil.

That was gallant. "No fresh horse should be wasted on anyone but a militiaman," said Sybil. Jane was already drinking at the trough, with Sybil still on her back.

"Stay here by the fire," Mistress Carver invited Sybil again. "I'll ride on to the others. When you've had a rest, you can ride home."

But that would have taken Sybil back through the mills and Big Pond, where soldiers must now be truly swarming the roads.

She said simply, "Mistress Carver, I'll be faster than you."

"Yes." Mistress Carver dropped her head and said, "I'd be a fool to think I could match you! Well, I guess I don't mind so much being old as I mind being gray and old!"

"Ma, you're not gray and old," said Barney, darting up to kiss her.

Sybil grinned.

"I will be before this is over," Mistress Carver said. "If only I could—"

"It's all right," Sybil interrupted. "I know the route. I'm already delaying. . . ." She picked up the reins and backed a little from the door.

Timmy dashed out and pressed a johnnycake into her hand. He gripped her cold, wet fingers in his warm, dry ones. Somehow it made Sybil feel more confident. She would have expected Timmy's—Timothy's!—hand to be clammy and nervous the way the rest of him seemed—but maybe anyone's hand would have comforted her now. "Godspeed!" she said.

"Same to you, Syb." So calm. How brave. Who'd have thought it?

She left him behind her and rode on.

Billy Hill's house . . . Izzy Pinckney's (she warned his mother that she had used her as an alibi at Big

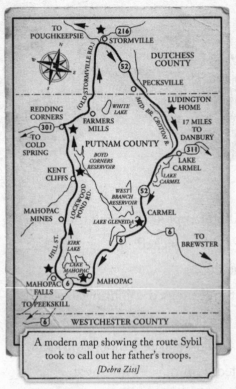

A modern map showing the route Sybil
took to call out her father's troops.
[Debra Ziss]

Pond) . . . Captain Hitchcock . . . Master Morris . . . on and on Sybil rode, climbing the long hill and entering the dark fog of the marshes at its back.

Here the houses were too far apart to extend the chain of alarm. They'd only wake if Sybil waked them. Sybil knew which doors to thump on with her stick and where it was wise to yell as well. She knew where *not* to stop, and where not to even slow. And she could be reasonably certain that, despite the drama of her announcement, the militiamen in the houses she awakened would know enough about their neighbors to keep a cool head in their midst.

If they were careful, if they were wise, if they were ready, they could be out and gone before the Loyalists among them could try to stop them.

CHAPTER 17

—— *One thirty in the morning* ——

Sybil rode as if she didn't care anymore, the terror of Big Pond far behind, the long uphill from the Carvers' house to the marshes conquered. She was farther than halfway now, with most of the regiment awakened and, as she imagined them, pulling out their coats and hats, strapping on their knapsacks and their muskets, gathering knives and rifles and whatever they had as weapons, and kissing their wives and children good-bye.

She thought of Timmy Carver, old enough to wed if only anyone would have him, kissing his mother good-bye. What Sybil was doing now was hard and could end in tragedy any moment. But it was better, Sybil felt, than staying home. She couldn't. What kind of Patriot would she be if she did? What kind of Daughter of Liberty?

She sighed, thinking of Enoch. What better hero was there than someone who'd let other people think wrong things about him in order to help his country?

But those were dangerous thoughts. Enoch! Spit on the ground. Where was he now? Going north, to spread the news of the latest British invasion, to prepare northern New Yorkers for the possibility that the British would march next to meet the troops stationed in Canada.

She thought of sweet, brave Hannah, catching up with Enoch and hiking north, camping in the woods, and a flash of jealousy went through her. But in the next moment, she knew that she wouldn't have gone with Enoch. Not with the Seventh Regiment being called up to go off to fight their own battle. Not with her own chance at making a difference hanging in the balance.

She wished Hannah and Enoch invisibility, dry weather, food, and kindness from people along the way, and a new, safe place.

Here, where Sybil rode, the only invisibility came

from a night as dark as pitch. She was riding toward the remotest corner of the county, and once she'd reached it, she'd have to ride on toward home, back into the thick of things.

Along the river everything was wet. The rain beat on the water and ground as loud as a drum. At any other time, the riverbank would have been the riskiest part, the road so near on the left side to the rushing water, full of spring rain with more every minute, and the woods to the right a black abyss and very likely concealing watchers.

If anybody saw Sybil, she never knew. There may have been Cow Boys. Skinners. Rascals and demons. If they lurked waiting, if they saw the hoof splash in the puddle or the glimmer of her eye, if they reached out to grab, Sybil and Lady Jane whistled through them like wind in the trees, without warning and gone without a trace.

───────── *Two o'clock* ─────────

Sybil didn't know who was going to fall apart first, herself or Lady Jane. Poor Jane's tongue was nearly hanging out, her breath heaving through her shoulders

under Sybil's weight. Sybil gentled her knees against Jane's withers in a hug. She knew she couldn't have taken one of the Carvers' horses, and yet . . . if Jane slowed too much, how would the rest of the regiment get the word about the muster?

The road to Foshay's Corner was really just a track past two houses, hardly worth the trouble, but there was no other way of getting through the swamp. It was a crucial part of the route.

The two privates who'd signed on with the militia—Benjamin Knapp and William Wright—were both farmers with young children and no farmhands, work-ing pretty little plots Papa practically had to hound them into leaving. Sybil pounded on their doors any-way and gave her alarm with as much fear of God as she could summon up. Papa had said you couldn't count on anyone on the route after these two. Both Hasbrouck brothers on the next two farms had refused to sign the Patriot pledge.

She slowed the mare and turned her into the soft mud at the edge of the lane to muffle her hooves. If she could just make it to Finch Gildersleeve's house, she'd soon reach the turning for the Storms', then the Pecks', then down the long hill home.

When she caught the movement coming toward her from the barn under the trees—it would have been white in daylight but now it barely showed—her first response was fury with herself. Caught daydreaming, caught slowing down, caught taking her time, she might as well have been caught napping! Stupid! Useless!

This narrow road was useless, too, a stupid trap for stupid girls. There was nowhere to run but a swamp with a river beyond, or a house where a Tory lived, or back the way she came. Going back was the only option.

Sybil dug her heels into Lady Jane and pulled the reins hard right, and spun the horse around. Not fast enough! Jane pulled up with a loud cry.

They were caught by a man much too big to be meddled with. He was as tall as the horse, with a face dark in these shadows under the brim of a black hat. The road behind him was blocked by a horse standing across it. He held Lady Jane by her halter. The hemp of it rasped Sybil's hand as she fought for control. For the first time, she felt a scream grow in her throat, while wondering who on earth was there to hear it. She couldn't help it; her voice rose and—

"Hush, Mistress Ludington!" said the deep voice. "I've brought thee a fresh horse."

It was Peaceable Moon, deep in the northern backwoods, populated sparsely by Loyalist and rebel and Indian, out in the harshest part of night, asking to take her sweet mare. "Jane is fine" was all she managed to say in one raspy exhale.

"Jane is exhausted," said Peaceable. "There is a friend nearby with a stall for her. Star has been waiting to take her place."

Sybil nudged Jane, but Peaceable was too strong for

them both. "Mistress Ludington, would I harm thy father's daughter?"

She pulled away, but again he stopped her. "Would I harm Hannah's friend?"

She sighed in exasperation and fear. "Hannah is gone! What does it matter?"

She didn't care if he was surprised by that. Thinking of Hannah made her think of Enoch, and thinking of Enoch reminded her of what he'd said one time: *A person needs to study whatever's in front of him to see what it really is.*

"Hannah sent me to find you," said Peaceable. "Would I leave my Star with thee if I meant thee or thy horse any harm?"

"I have to go, Mister Moon!" said Sybil.

"Take Star," said Peaceable.

She did. She dropped her stick and slid from Jane's back, hugged her horse's head, and let Peaceable boost her into Star's saddle and shorten the stirrups to fit.

"I'll bring Jane back tomorrow," the Quaker said.

"How old are you, Mister Moon?" she asked.

"Seventeen," he said.

"You could join the regiment yourself," she said.

In the dim light, she saw him smile. She didn't wait for him to say he couldn't offer an opinion.

"Maybe in a way you have joined," she said.

"Take care," he said.

Sybil rode the rest of her route with Star.

———————— *Three o'clock* ————————

Sybil took the turn toward the Storms' at a gallop. The houses where the Storm family lived were close together here, shoulder to shoulder. She knew which ones to avoid, but they'd all hear her news quick enough. She banged on the first door as if trying to wake them all at once, calling out, and dashing on to the next door on the route without waiting for the first to open up. Down the narrow, sleeping street she went, loud enough to wake the dead.

A door opened when the stick was cocked but hadn't struck yet. Sybil narrowly missed smashing Finch Gildersleeve in the face. She must have been shocked, because he simply slipped the stick from her hand and stood there in his nightshirt, gaping up at her.

Gildersleeve didn't have to look up much. He was

tall, with the kind of shoulders that came from work-
ing in the forge. He would have lost a beauty contest
with a scarecrow.

"Ludington sent his *lass*?" said Gildersleeve as she
lunged for the stick. He kept it away with one hand,
twisted it through Star's reins to hold him, and, as if all
this was no trouble, wrapped the other hand nearly all the
way around her thigh, just above the knee and moving
higher.

She'd heard Papa and Mama argue about Finch.
"Can't help it what he's like, I need him," Papa claimed.
Mama said he wasn't to be trusted, but Sybil had never
been able to decide why. "He's crazy the way you need in
a battle," Papa had said. Not crazy-smart like a fox.
Finch Gildersleeve was crazy-vicious and ambitious, she
thought, like a lone wolf trying to push out a pack leader.

Gildersleeve might expose the regiment to other
risks than the ones that ran through Sybil's head now.
She thought she knew what Mama had meant. She knew
some tricks to defend herself against men, involving feet,
boots, and knees, but Papa needed Finch. . . .

She leaned toward him now and whispered, "You
know something, Mister Gildersleeve?" Lightning
snapped overhead.

"Mistress Ludington?" he said in a wolfish growl.

She was nerve-wrackingly close to his gleaming eyes. "There's an officer position Papa's been considering."

"Ah," said Gildersleeve, his thumb caressing her leg.

"I wouldn't want to have to tell him anything to turn him aside from you."

"You wouldn't have to, sweetheart," said Finch, and leaned in close to her. She put her hand on his wrist, held it tight, and as he neared, she jerked her knee up through the stick, breaking it. Star's reins fell loose, and she snapped them up.

Gildersleeve jumped toward her with a snarl.

"Sorry! The British are burning Danbury! Muster at Ludington's!" Sybil shouted. The thunder crackled around her as she charged off into the dark and the fresh downpour that swallowed her out of his view.

———————— *Four o'clock* ————————

The night is darkest just before the dawn. That's what people said, and Sybil was in a position to confirm it.

She was wet and exhausted, with black snakes of hair slapping her face, on a horse the color of the tar she'd be covered with if she got caught by the Tories, the clothes plastered on her legs, and a soreness building between her and Star, rubbing worse every time the horse's hooves landed.

At the top of the highest hill above Oliver Peck's house, Sybil asked herself what compelled people to live this far from civilization, yet she was grateful to see a dim light in the tavern there.

She slowed Star and battered the door with her fist, knowing she'd give someone inside a fright but past worrying about such manners. Hezekiah Peck—born a Tory, and hoping to die a Tory—would get the news, too, but Sybil couldn't help that. It was too late to worry about rousing the wrong people.

A face came to the window, some old ghost who'd been nodding at the hearth. Sybil shouted her warning and rode on.

She'd done it. The tavern keeper would get the word out. Horse and rider trotted over the hilltop road. Sybil lifted her eyes to meet a thin orange light that edged a field to her left, the east. Here comes the sun, storm and all, she thought. Then she realized: it's not the sun. It's the fire! Fifteen miles in the distance, Danbury was burning.

CHAPTER 18

By dawn, there was a mass of hundreds of soldiers on the parade ground up the hill from the Ludingtons' house. The family inside could hear the rumble of their deep voices, the clank and click of the muskets and powder horns strapped over their shoulders, the scuff of their boots as they idled over the parade ground, pacing the way men do, keeping warm and talking, mostly quietly—with occasional bursts into bragging and promises, threats and cussing.

Archie was at the upstairs window watching them. It looked like a parade was about to happen. Drums lined up along the grass edge of the ground, the officers in their new blue coats, and the militiamen in shades

Soldiers of the Continental Army infantry, 1779 to 1783. *[LC-USZC4-2135]*

of rust and white and gray—homespun, home-woven, home-sewn farm shirts or buckskin shirts and breeches—and boots better suited for horseback than walking as far as these men would have to walk today. They had so much to carry: their knapsacks with blankets and tents, a haversack for food, knife cases to strap to their sides, muskets, and more.

Their horses, tied along the rail, pawed the ground and must have wondered what was happening. They wanted to get going, too. But Papa looked over his shoulder. Sybil wasn't yet back.

A horse's hooves pounded along the road toward the Ludingtons' front door. Molly knew it wasn't Papa's horse, Sir Kay; he and Kay wouldn't be coming that fast from the parade ground. But it wasn't Lady Jane, either. Mama stood up, baby Abigail clutched tightly to her chest, her eyes on Molly. Molly shouldered the musket awkwardly; it was way too big for her, but she tried to be game.

Mama opened the door just wide enough for her head to peek out; even so, a spray of wind and rain burst past her into the hall. With a jolt, she yelled, "Sybil!"

All the breath went out of Molly. She dropped the musket in the corner, pulled Mama back into the dry hall, and ran to meet her sister. Sybil came bounding up like a haunted thing, wet hair flying out on all sides, sodden clothes pasted to her arms and legs. She was on a strange horse—a black horse, wild-eyed, wet mane flopped over a white diamond on its forehead.

Sybil threw down the reins. "Put him up, Molly, please."

"Whose is he?"

She didn't answer. She grabbed the saddle horn and threw her leg over the back of the horse. Molly saw her lurch and caught her coming down, the reins in a tangle, her knees giving way.

Mama hauled her up and got her inside to the big chair in front of the fire. Molly returned from the stable and grabbed the kettle, and Mama began stripping off the streaming clothes. Behind them, Archie held the baby. Sybil reached for the mug of ale that Mama offered, took a sip, and breathed out. "I rode all the way," she said.

"Rest a minute before you tell us," said Mama.

"You did it, Sybil," said Molly. "The soldiers are here."

In the parade ground, a drum began—Abram's deep-voiced one—and was joined by the Townsend boys' and Jeremiah's. At some unspoken command, Papa and his officers swung into their saddles and started along the road to Quaker Hill and Danbury beyond.

Mama, Sybil, Molly, Archie, and the little boys— Hank, Derick, Turtle—stood at the front door. They stood there until the last soldier was gone.

It was a long time before they were absolutely sure they had stopped hearing those drums.

It was another long time—after Sybil had at last fallen asleep in the chair by the fire—before the sound

This painting, known as both *Yankee Doodle* and *The Spirit of '76*, depicts the troops of the Continental Army marching into battle.
[LC-DIG-ppmsca-05936]

of a wagon came along the road. The wagon had a big black horse pulling it, and a chestnut mare tied behind.

In the wagon was the big, blond Quaker man.

Molly threw her arms around Jane, relieved to see someone she loved again and to hide her face from Peaceable. Archie and Mama came out the door behind her.

"We thank you truly, Peaceable," said Mama,

whispering to keep from waking Sybil. "The troops moved out faster because Sybil had Star."

"But, Peaceable," Molly said, "what's going to happen if General Tryon catches up with you?"

"I can offer no opinion," he said, and winked.

He got up onto his wagon, Star and Moon together again in front. He drove out of their yard and toward Quaker Hill, following the muddy hoofprints and footfalls of Papa's regiment of four hundred men.

"Mistress Prosser could cause trouble for him," Mama said. "She'll get Doctor Prosser back eventually—he's too mean to die!—and then he'll make even more of a ruckus about the Ludingtons than he did before."

It would be three years before any of them caught sight of Enoch again. By that time, he had helped Hannah map the way to Vermont and had said good-bye to her in the mountains north of Albany. Whether she reached freedom, they would never know.

Sybil said, "I would have gone north with him, too, Mama."

"I know, my love," said Mama.

<hr />

The day after Sybil's ride, they did the chores. Despite the prestorm work they had done all day yesterday—was it only yesterday?—they cooked and cleaned still more, and fed and watered and slopped and walked and weeded and weaved and sewed.

They waited, in the way of women and children everywhere, to see what would come next out of the dark maze that was the world: Death? Fire? Or their own dear ones?

When someone came, it wasn't who they thought it would be, some messenger.

It was Becky.

She came running up the hill in the late afternoon, her hem muddied, her hair ragged and falling down, looking as if she had run crying all the way from the Hazens'. She fell into Mama's arms.

"Is it Leazar?" Mama asked.

Becky sobbed, "He's fine!"

"What?" Sybil, kneeling at her side, gaped across at Mama and Molly. They all had their arms around Becky. Archie and the little boys stood in an outer ring, as still as statues.

"Then who?" said Mama in a harsh, frightened voice.

"Just—just Leazar!" wailed Becky. "He—I'll never marry him!"

"Why?" Molly asked.

"He ran off!"

"Where?"

"Home!" She waited for them to understand. "He came back while the rest went on."

Mama exhaled with a moan and a sigh.

"He deserted," Becky said, her voice anguished. "While his brother went on . . . while Papa went on . . . while the rest of the regiment went on . . . Eleazar Hazen went off and hid in the swamp."

CHAPTER 19

APRIL 27–28, 1777

In the middle of the night, the British soldiers had found the American stock of rum in a warehouse in Danbury. While they packed carts with the supplies they wanted and hauled out and burned those that wouldn't keep, it seemed like a pity to waste good rum. So they got good and drunk, and then they got lazy and violent.

Moving supplies to a bonfire was too time-consuming; in the interest of efficiency, they burned down the storage barns and everything in them. The streets ran greasy with melted pork fat. The town was filled with a strange odor of burned sugar, mixed with the smell of torched woolen blankets and canvas tents.

General Tryon fought for control, and when he got it, he moved the troops out with all the briskness he could summon—which wasn't much considering the activities of the night.

General Arnold spent the night a mile from Danbury in Bethel, Connecticut. He was up all night worrying, waiting to see which way the redcoats would go. He fired off coded messages across the New York border to General McDougall in Peekskill and John Jay in Fishkill. Arnold thought the redcoats would march toward the Hudson River. But if Tryon had ever intended to march toward the Hudson, he changed his mind now.

Tryon set a goal to retreat to his ships, which sat just offshore at Compo Beach, but it was no use going back the way he had come, since all the towns along the way were waiting for them to return. Scouts in the woods were ready to run in any direction. A move to the east by Tryon would be countered by one from Patriot Generals Arnold and Silliman. Tryon decided to climb the steep hillside to Ridgefield, then try his luck passing over the road that ran south to the shore from there.

Arnold and Silliman ran up the west side of the ridge and built a barrier of logs and carts and furniture across Ridgefield's main street, with woods on one side and a cliff on the other. Ten miles from the barrier, the third Patriot general, David Wooster, caught up with the British and attacked them from the rear. His troops fired on the redcoats, they replied with cannon, and General Wooster himself fell from his horse, mortally wounded.

David Wooster, who lived from 1711 to 1777. *[LC-USZ62-3621]*

Then Colonel Ludington's regiment joined in the rout.

Hidden in the trees above and shooting from behind stone walls and wells and tree trunks, they harassed the British and rushed them up against the barricade.

The British soldiers and the Continental soldiers did not fight by the same rules. The British thought opposing sides should line up across a battlefield from one another: *ready, aim, fire*. Those who fell were stepped over. Again: *ready, aim, fire*, hold your position, keep marching forward. The soldiers who made it to the far side of the battlefield were the winners.

But there weren't enough Patriot soldiers to fight that way. For them, the land they fought on wasn't just a battlefield; it was home, and if you were going to take it, it would be over their cold, dead bodies. So they did what they had to do to keep it: they hid, snuck, spied, and shot. And if someone was bearing down on them, they didn't hold their positions; they ran. This was especially true of the militiamen, whose profession was farming, not soldiering.

Experienced soldiers like Benedict Arnold and Colonel Ludington became frustrated by this dashing about. Left standing alone, they wound up having to dash for cover themselves, then chase around the woods gathering up stray men so they could mount another attack.

Colonel Ludington and General Arnold and General Silliman attacked over and over all day. That night they camped in the woods. In the morning they resumed fighting as the British beat a retreat to the sea.

In a last hurrah, British soldiers waiting aboard ship piled onto the beach and marched by the hundreds to mount a counterattack. The Patriots charged after them, backing them down the beach toward the water.

At last the redcoats escaped on their ships. Under Patriot fire, they abandoned Compo Beach and sailed back to New York.

Then Benedict Arnold and his troops, and General Silliman and his troops, and General Wooster's men and Colonel Ludington's Seventh Regiment of the Dutchess County militia marched back home.

———◦◦◦◦———

They came straggling home in ones and twos.

The Ludingtons didn't see many of them, but the few who headed north—the Pecks and the Storms and their neighbors—came up the hill and paused at the house to get a drink and pay their respects to Mama before rushing home to their families and their fields.

Each soldier's arrival carried news that hurt the Ludingtons to the core, news of lives lost, blood lost, broken bones, broken hearts. In a way, the worst were the early comers who skulked past without stopping; some might have called them deserters.

Some of those who did stop called themselves the smart ones. "The idea of staying in place while men run at you with guns and knives!" said one fellow.

"My children won't eat next winter if I don't get those seeds in the furrows now," said another man.

"I've got too much at stake to be somebody's scarecrow!" said another father who stopped to drink.

The Ludingtons waited endless hours. It got sunny and warm. When Sybil pushed up her sleeves, Mama said, "It's just that it's the first really hot day. By July, you'll be used to it." If Papa didn't come back today, what would happen to his family by July?

Sybil banged out the back door and dashed for the paddock and the animals, trying not to fall apart. Suddenly Molly was behind her, both arms around her from the back.

"Come on," Sybil said. "Let's go."

"Where?"

"To meet Papa. I can't sit here one minute longer."

"You think we'll find him?" Molly asked incredulously. What did they know about where Papa was, or even if he was alive?

They saddled up Lady Jane. Then, once again, there were two sisters pounding down the road toward Shaw's Pond. Pale blue sky, baby green leaves sprouting almost as they passed, unfolding in the warm air. Sybil avoided the marsh of Horse Pound Road and took the main road instead, reasoning that this was the way the men would come home from the Ridgefield road.

Nightmare scenes came into Sybil's head: Papa lying dead along a shore-bound road. Papa dead in a cart coming home. Papa wounded, carried along on

Sir Kay's back. Kay shot out from under him, Papa walking, limping.

Suddenly she knew where to go first. Solomon Hopkins was at work in his pea patch, his cane at his elbow, a broad hat on his head. He straightened up calmly as though people bounding into his yard on horseback was a regular occurrence. "Mister Hopkins! What news?" Sybil called.

"News? The dashing Miss Sybil."

"Papa—" she breathed, more a prayer than a question.

"No," said Solomon. "Nothing yet."

"Any news at all?" said Molly. "Are the British coming back? Are they coming up the Hudson?"

"They might yet," said Solomon. "But not now. No, sweet, it's Timothy Carver."

"Oh no," said Sybil. Molly leaned against Lady Jane.

Sybil felt a horrible jolt of sympathy for Timmy.

"Where?" she asked, wanting to add to her picture of the succession of skirmishes along the road back to Compo, needing more information to add to her timeline that would bring Papa back by this day or that, depending on what happened when.

"Near Keeler's Tavern," said Solomon. "He was one of those waiting in the trees beyond the barricade." When the girls said nothing, he went on. "No, he wasn't playing to strength. He's not the sort of person you'd expect to hide up a tree like a sleeping owl."

Sybil blinked. "Poor Timmy," she said.

Solomon pressed his hand to his chest. "Dear Sybil. Eleazar Hazen brought him home."

"But Leazar deserted!" Molly burst out.

"He went back," said Solomon. "He meant to follow your father after all."

"Better late than never," said Sybil harshly.

"Better indeed," said Solomon. "When he heard Timmy had fallen from the tree, he went and found him and took him to his mother."

Silently she left Solomon in his garden, got on Jane, and pulled Molly up behind. They rode away.

It seemed that everyone else could be gone in a moment.

The road was a blur beneath Lady Jane's hooves. Sybil pushed the mare to a gallop, following the path she'd taken what seemed to be a hundred years ago—past the Hazens' to Belden's Bridge. They passed through Red Mills in a cloud of dust, the mud summer-dry already. They didn't pause, didn't worry, didn't care. Nobody tried to stop them.

Sybil must have turned at the mills and headed up the broad hill, but never remembered it afterward. The world was crazy and wrong if someone honest, true, and good like Timmy could be taken as he fought for a country that was born for freedom and peace!

Sybil watched the Carvers' house grow near— forgetting the horse beneath her, forgetting they were the ones on the move. The doors were ajar, the windows thrown open in the warmth of day. Mistress Carver's peonies had huge pink buds. Voices came through the windows—women in the house and men in the yard behind. Sybil pulled Lady Jane up short; you didn't go charging into the yard of someone in mourning. Stately, silently, they headed for the paddock, then Jane let out a whinny.

Sir Kay stood tied to the rail, and through the door, Sybil heard her father's voice.

EPILOGUE

Later, they would say it was a triumph that in the Battle of Ridgefield, the Patriots lost only twelve.

Only twelve! Twelve might be nothing in the larger scheme of the war. It might be a small number of casualties for a battle that may have saved the Hudson River from British domination. But if someone you loved was one of those twelve, it was no small number at all. It was twelve too many. Just one would be too many, if the one was the one you loved.

Sybil Ludington saw a scene in her head that she could never tell anyone, although she was sure others imagined it, too: Timmy hiding behind the stone fence with his brother and his father, as directed by Sybil's

Papa. *Get back there under cover and take a shot as soon as you're able.* She saw Timmy, who always tried to do everything better than Barney, leap up to climb the tree.

In a few more days the budded maples would have bloomed, dropping red buds all over the stone wall. A few more weeks and the leaves would have been large enough to hide the boy in the trees. A few more steps along the road, and the redcoat Timmy aimed at would have stood at a different angle, so he wouldn't have had a clear shot at Timmy.

Instead, she saw Timmy get hit—not killed, just wounded, and shocked enough to lose his balance. She saw him drop from the tree. She saw his head bang against the stone, saw him fall into the myrtle and poison ivy and prickers behind the wall. She saw him go still and silent.

The evening that Papa came home, he said, "Whatever else Leazar did, he went back for his countrymen and stayed for his friend."

Becky said, "I wouldn't have left you, Papa."

Papa studied the back of his own hands, resting—so tired—on the tabletop. Becky laid her hand on one of his and added, "Family business, Papa."

"Family business," said Tertullus, and smacked the table. Nobody else said anything. Mama patted Turtle's hand.

Papa said, "It was chaos, Rebecca. It was loud and fast and terrible. I gathered up all I could, and so did Silliman and Arnold, and I couldn't look back to see who fell behind me."

"Or ran off," said Becky in a whisper.

"He went *back*," Sybil insisted. She had thought that Leazar would be a brother. Now Timmy was gone, and Leazar was rejected.

Papa lifted his eyes to Becky's. "Forgive him, my dear," he said.

"Eventually I will," said Becky. "But marry him I will not."

<hr />

It would be years before Sybil stopped waiting for Enoch. He stayed where nobody knew him until it was finally safe. Maybe he kept her waiting too long, because they both married someone else and—typical of both of them—there was no explanation.

Even when the war ended, and America won its

independence from Great Britain, many people did not feel—like Peaceable—that it was safe to offer an opinion. What if the British came back—as they tried to do in the War of 1812—and persecuted the Patriots?

Enoch's doings didn't come to light until years later, when he testified about his spy work in order to win a pension (support money) from the new government.

Sybil's ride was kept even quieter. While the Revolution was still raging, it may have seemed safest to stay in the shadows. Like many courageous women, Sybil's wartime activities were hushed up while the heroic deeds of men went down in history.

More than a hundred years later, two of Henry Ludington's grandchildren wrote a biography of their grandfather. In it, they retold a family story—the one that told of Sybil's ride. The details had been lost to history, but that didn't stop many people from filling in the blanks, and others from treating their imaginings as facts. Many pieces of information about Sybil—for instance, that her horse was called Star—have been perpetuated without proof.

According to the grandchildren, Sybil rode alone over forty miles around Dutchess County (now Putnam County) to call out the militia to muster before the Battle of Ridgefield. That is all that is really known. The rest is—and always will be—family business.

AUTHOR'S NOTE

Filling in the blanks is necessary in order to flesh out Sybil's story.

The skeleton of the story is the history of battles and life in Dutchess, Westchester, and Fairfield Counties during the American Revolution. It's true that George Washington and John Jay were the brains behind many intelligence schemes and spy rings. The codes and secret message techniques included here were used by them. The participation of Colonel Henry Ludington's Seventh Regiment in different battles and wartime activities is well documented and forms another part of this story's framework.

Many of the characters in this story are based on people who really lived at this time—including Doctor

Prosser, whose men surrounded the Ludington house and were fooled by shadows, and Solomon Hopkins, who left an upstairs window open in case Enoch Crosby needed a refuge. Margaret Corbin, the first woman to draw a military pension in recognition of her bravery at the Battle of Fort Washington, is also mentioned and might have been an inspiration to the real Sybil. Their stories endure here with a grain of salt: these began as oral histories, and have no doubt changed in the telling.

Although Solomon Hopkins, the Hazens, the Carvers, and others appear on the roster of Ludington's regiment, little is known about them. I invented their personalities, relationships, and activities, including Eleazar Hazen's desertion and Timmy's death. Although events like these happened during this battle, we don't know what really happened to these people.

Hannah and Peaceable are made-up characters, but they represent types of people who lived in Dutchess County during the Revolution. So many were part of what happened behind the scenes during this war—including women, African Americans, servants, and Quakers—that I wanted to suggest their importance in history.

Much of what is told here about Enoch Crosby is true, including the story of how he became a double agent. He was known to have been a friend to Henry Ludington, and there are stories of him sharing codes with the

Ludington daughters. There is no evidence of a real romance between him and Sybil, but it seemed to me that he would have been a hero to her and maybe more.

Sybil Ludington 🏵 *Youthful Heroine*

A stamp from 1975 dedicated to Sybil Ludington. *[United States Postal Service]*

Sybil and Becky were known to be good shots with muskets and to patrol their family home. The tale of Prosser's men hiding in the woods comes from the family biography, as does a later scene (not in this book) in which Colonel Ludington catches up to Prosser and confronts him, horse whip in hand.

Enoch settled down near his parents' farm. Sybil grew up and married Edmund Ogden and moved to Catskill, New York, where people didn't talk about her or make conjectures about her secrets. When Edmund took ill and died in 1799, she held things together for her son Henry's sake, running a tavern on her own and taking no guff from farmer, trader, or trapper. Same old Sybil.

Edmund had fought in the militia during the American Revolution. After his death, when it came time to apply for a pension in 1838, Sybil couldn't produce the papers that proved their marriage. So she, who had mustered the militia for a key battle, was left in poverty.

With nothing to live on, Sybil went home to the house on the hill above Shaw's Pond and ran the farm for Mama and Papa until their deaths, and afterward, until her own.

Historians searching for women's contributions give a number of reasons that their deeds are lost to posterity: first, maybe women weren't looking for recognition, honor, or fame; they didn't want the attention—good or bad—that could come from talking about their activities or heroism. Second, in these times, it wasn't always wise to come down too clearly on either side; who knew which side would ultimately dominate, and then what would happen to the doers of deeds? (Of course, this particular problem was shared by men.) Third, women were second-class citizens. Along with Quakers, servants, and slaves, their deeds didn't matter as much—but maybe that gave them an edge. Who would believe, after all, that a sixteen-year-old girl could ride forty miles to bring out a four-hundred-man militia, all in one night? I do. Do you?

A statue commemorating Sybil Ludington stands in Carmel, New York.
[Anthony22 at the English language Wikipedia]

ACKNOWLED...

I owe a debt to Mark Allan Baker's books about espiona[ge]
and a lecture he gave about it at Byrd's Books in my home-
town, Bethel, Connecticut.

I am grateful to Sallie Sypher, the deputy historian of
Putnam County (which used to be part of Dutchess
County), for her detailed response to my manuscript and
assistance with research.

I stood on the shoulders of Vincent D'Acquino as I
tried to understand Sybil's life. Jonathan Churchill ad-
vised me about Revolutionary War musical instruments
and their role in battles.

And my favorite historians, Mark Young and Bethany
Pinho, gave me the benefit of their imagination and in-
sight as we retraced Sybil's heroic route.